Lovably Broken

SYLVIA AER

Infinity Dreamt Books

Published by Infinity Dreamt

Website: www.infinitydreamt.tk

ISBN: 978-0-9916914-7-0

ONE

Now

I'm not the only one in the room, but I'm grateful when I feel like I am. Another human being sleeps a few feet away, but he may as well be a ghost.

I force myself to sit up on the small twin bed that is situated near the couch. I look over to our makeshift living room that has a simple brown coffee table and a floor lamp in the corner. I wake all too often hoping that Phil is not here. It matters not to me whether it is morning or night because my routine has become too insignificant to matter. I sleep to avoid him. I sleep to dream of a better place and what my life might be like without him. I pray for a lot of things, yet God has yet to answer me on this one.

He is still asleep, as I watch his chest rise and fall slowly, and I use the moment to tip-toe out of bed and make my way to the bathroom. Locking the door behind me, I turn around and look at my reflection in the bathroom mirror. My dark brown strands of hair are dry and lifeless. My eyes, sometimes a light blue, sometimes a light green, are framed by dark circles. Today they are almost brown. I wonder if they have taken on a new color to match my feelings. I'm as pale as death, so I turn on the tap and splash some cold water on my face. I feel a bit better. Not enough to push forward into the evening, but here and alive-like for a moment.

A loud knocking hits the bathroom door.

"Wait a minute!" I shout back. He is already shouting and swearing at me. One word gets through; work. I had been wondering what time it was. I skip using the toilet and open the door, and he pushes past me as if every last minute counts for him. I look at the clock in the hallway. It is persistent to remain fifteen minutes behind, regardless of how often I change the battery or adjust it. Like me, it too stubbornly refuses to move forward.

I walk past the kitchen, pondering whether to wash the piling dishes. It matters little if I do or I don't. The only other one to ever see them is Phil, and even if I were to return to being a doting maid, I still wouldn't hear the end of his scorn. I walk back to my bed. It's the one place in the tiny apartment that I can almost call my own. I'm happy to have wakened up at this hour because within minutes he will be gone. Then I will have the entire apartment to myself and its safety in loneliness. Soon enough, the front door slams and silence remains. My thoughts grow just as silent and blank as the white wall before me. For the next ten hours, I am free. Free to do absolutely nothing.

TWO

Now

I decide to try my luck and sneak outside of the apartment the next day. I'm feeling more energetic than usual this late afternoon. I'm unsure about whether it's fear or excitement that drives me. It's likely a combination of both. I've been without junk food for over two weeks, so I'm on the hunt. The bakery section in the grocery store spans out before me like a field of endless sugar. But as much as I would like to take just a bit of everything, my wallet is thin. I open my small, pink change purse, and count the few toonies and loonies that I have within, along with accounting for my health card. I tell myself that one day I will go to the doctor and ask her just what is wrong with me, but not today. Today I have no more than an hour before the man returns from his sports and drinking outing at his friend's house.

My eyes lock onto the pecan tarts. It's an instant winner, as next to being my favorite, it's also on sale. I reach out to pick up a package when I feel something grab my arm, and then my hand. It all happens so fast that it takes me a second to realize that my wallet has just been stolen right out of my hand. I spin around and look just in time to see the thief run out of the grocery store and into the parking lot.

I speed off after him, bumping into an old man on the way out almost hard enough to topple him. I call back an apology as I run at full speed for outside. There are enough cars around to keep me looking for days, and several are leaving. I don't know where to start looking. All I have is a flash of short, dark hair to go on. I feel like crying and screaming all at the same time, but I stay quiet. My single piece of ID is gone. My money is gone. And my time is up as I should have been home by now. I scan the cars one more time, before sucking in my anger and starting for home.

It starts to rain as I see my apartment building in the distance. I'm clearly a magnet for misery at this point. Or I'm cursed. My home for the last ten years is a rundown apartment building that looks more like a castle that has survived the Medieval times. I look up at some of the windows that now have a black frame painted from smoke. The brown bricks can only be falling off one by one. Maintenance is on the bottom of this place's priorities. They're too busy trying to keep up with the security.

A drop of water hits my eye, followed by a heavier downpour. The rain puts a serious damper on my original plan. I wanted to sneak out, buy a snack, and return without him ever suspecting I left. Now I look like a drowned rat that just crawled out of the sewer. I jog up to the front of my building, before slowing on seeing someone standing in front of the doors. He's sporting a leather jacket and tidy black jeans, and his dark hair stands out as familiar. My pink change purse is in the man's hands. I look around fearfully for a black van that might pull up to kidnap me next.

"Why don't you call for help?" the criminally handsome man asks as I approach.

My thief is taunting me, but his voice is not as loud as the clock ticking inside my head. I don't have time to wrestle with a possibly crazy man, as good looking as he is or not. I turn and make my way around the building. It's my luck as a stranger leaves, holding the otherwise locked back door open for me. I dash inside and make my way to the elevators. I wait for one to come down, and wipe a drop of water from my forehead. I enter the first elevator to arrive and head down the hall to my apartment door on arriving on my floor. I steel myself and slowly open my door. I let out the longest breath of relief when I look into the living room to find that the man has passed out in his drunken state on the couch. Phew. For now. I open the door the rest of the way before a shouting stops me in my tracks. I look down the hall to see that the crazy man is still after me. I rush into my apartment and quietly close and lock the door. Safe. Or at least I am for a moment before his loud knocking hits the door. I contemplate shouting at the guy to get lost, but it's too late as the drunk on the couch stirs and then wakes up.

"Where were you?" Phil asks as he gets to his feet, then nearly falls over.

"I, uh...stepped out for some air." My lying could use some serious practice.

"Bullshit. Where were you really?" He's barely able to stay standing up in his drunken stupor.

The loud knocking hits the door again, and I flinch.

Phil heads over to the door and opens it, and glares at the taller man before him. "What do you want?"

"I just wanted to return this," the thief replies. The thief looks stunned by the sudden switch of faces before him. He's holding up my small pink wallet like a peace offering. "She dropped this on the sidewalk."

"Uh huh," Phil replies, unconvinced, and snatches it out of his hand. Then he throws it across the living room floor as if I'm supposed to fetch it. "So this is who you've been seeing?"

"What—?" I say in my defense, but it's unheard against his never-ending jealousy that I've never justified.

"Shut up you lying whore!" Phil shouts at me, then stomps my way.

I don't have time to react before his fist hits my face, sending everything around me into a violent spin until it all goes black.

THREE

Then

"Run!"

I don't know how I've ended up running like a madwoman; I only know that I'm sweating when I come to a sudden stop. The voice that shouted at me disappears into the trees, leaving me behind.

I turn around and try to get a sense of just where I am. It feels real, but I'm clearly in a dream when the woods suddenly vanish into thin air. With the trees gone, I'm left in a familiar driveway from my past. It becomes immediately apparent that this is no dream, but a nightmare.

"Get in the car, Aubree!"

My worker's voice hits me like a ragged-edged knife

across my spine. In the past, it was enough to get me into the car. My greatest fear was of appearing non-co-operative and never seeing my mother again.

"Aubree!"

"Go fuck yourself!" I yell back at her. She doesn't look to have taken it well as her face looks about ready to explode in a fury.

"You will never see your mother again, you just keep this up!" she threatens.

The threat means nothing as I already know how this story ends. I turn around and find the safety of the trees, and I start in a mad dash towards them. There was once a boy who used to wait for me in these woods. I still have to accept that I'm never going to see him again.

"Hey."

Another voice is trying to mess with me now, except it's coming from the real and all-powerful world. I look up through my waking haze to find my psycho stalker staring back at me. I'm in a strange bed, and he's sitting next to me. There should be a law that prevents insane people from being so gorgeous. Instead of screaming and trying to make a run for it, I'm stupid enough to stare at this beautiful cobra like some helpless prey. Now I'm victim to another guy. I'm feeling more hopeless than I started off as.

"What were you having a nightmare about?" he asks.

The question is unexpected, and it already feels like he's trying to distract me. My hand registers that it's touching soft, gray silk sheets.

"Who are you?" I ask.

He stands up and walks over to the kitchen. I sit up and look around. The place seems like some old warehouse converted into an expensive loft from the windows alone. The doors to the bedroom that I'm in are almost as wide as the wall that separates it from the living room. It's clean and modern, as the black leather sofas compliment the living room. The kitchen is mostly stainless steel and polished to magazine perfection. Expensive magazine perfection that is. My kidnapper has good taste. I'm impressed as my eyes register the precise location of the door and how many locks it has. He also has good taste in security. I've played this game before. First one to the door wins. This will be my greatest challenge yet, as my kidnapper is a good foot taller than me.

"How do you like your eggs?"

"Wha...?" I ask as I look from the door back to the kitchen. He is standing in front of the stove, confidently holding a spatula.

"That's if you're okay with...?"

"Scrambled," I reply, mostly by instinct. I'm starving. I'm an idiot when hungry.

He continues to cook and then brings me a plate of fluffy scrambled eggs and buttered toast.

Instead of thanking him, I eye it carefully, wondering if he's drugged my food.

"Eat up. I can't have you stay here forever."

I take a bite, and it's surprisingly good. I can't remember the last time that someone cooked for me. I'm scarfing down the contents of the plate before my mind snaps me back into a more civilized state. I swallow and offer a thank-you as I bring the plate to the sink.

"How's your head?" he asks.

I have enough calories in me now to register what he's talking about. I make my way over to the mirror next to the exit and look at my reflection. The bruise on the side of my face suggests that I look like I've been hit by a professional kickboxer. Or a train. Or both. I look like complete shit.

"I'm sorry about what happened. I had no idea that you were living with a psychopath," my cook says.

I blink as I look to where he goes to sit on the couch, setting a hot coffee cup on the table before him. Phil's punch to my face comes back to my memory. "It's not your fault. I shouldn't have tried to go out."

"You make it sound like your prisoner."

You have no idea. "Look, I appreciate you doing all

this, but I have to get back," I insist.

"Well, here's the thing, I didn't rescue you only to return you back to that drunken fool. I'll take you anywhere you want to go — except back to him. You have a friend or family member I can drive you to?"

I almost answer no, before thinking more on it. "I have a girlfriend who's just a couple blocks from Heddington Station." Please work this time, lying face of mine.

"Alright then," he says and gets to his feet. "You want a coffee before we go?"

"No thanks and I don't even know your name."

"It's Noah. And from what I read on your health card, you're Aubree, right?"

"Yeah. Why did you steal my wallet?" It clearly wasn't for money as I thought.

"I was looking for someone, and I assumed you were her."

The answer leaves my head spinning even more to just what this guy's deal is. "You have a weird way of getting a girl's attention."

"Well, it has always worked until now. I never had any girl I played the prank on get hurt. I'll have to rethink my strategy for the next time," Noah says.

He's just as bad of a liar as me, as it shows through his

face. I'm left to wonder to just how much of what he says is the truth. But I don't question him and follow him out and downstairs to his car. It's an old Dodge that looks like it survived several safaris among the lions before getting here. It's just the kind of car that you would throw a dead body into and push into a lake. Fear wakes up in me again, and it's screaming. Nope nope—not happening. "Ah, you know what, I can walk. I don't think I'm far from her place."

Noah sighs. "It's the car, isn't it?"

"No no, your car is great. I— "

"Just stop," he replies. "This lying to each other thing isn't working. You're just as bad as me. This is just my backup car. My brother took the more respectable-looking one. He's still restoring this one."

"Oh," I reply. He's right about the lying thing. I'm stumped for the first time to have competition.

As if summoned, a set of headlights flashes over my legs as another car pulls up next to the Dodge. It's a black Buick that is polished much like everything else in this man's life.

"Speak of the devil," Noah says as a man, just a tad shorter than he leaves the car. He has short blond hair and brown eyes that instantly paralyze me when he looks my way. I know this person.

"You found her...? Oh my god. Noah, you're a genius,"

the man says as he closes the car door and comes over to me.

My head is spinning faster now as there's something so familiar about him that it sends my heart racing at an incredible speed. It's all too much, too fast. For the first time in my life, I faint.

FOUR

Then

"I won't let them take you," Caleb says and looks in the direction of the forest path back to the house.

I've drifted into the past again in my sleep. "My knight in shining armor," I say, looking back at a younger Caleb. It's unreal with just how much of him I've forgotten. He's like a perfect painting that I have been allowed to see the entirety of again. His brown eyes fail to hide behind his messy blond bangs, and even if they could, I can always sense when he's looking my way. "That's cute, but you never met my worker." I ponder counting all the trees out here in the woods some day. In reality, I know that I will never be at this foster home long enough to give it a try. I lean back and more into him as he sits against the trunk behind him. Caleb wraps his arms around me, and I close my eyes, trying to use my willpower to make the future go away.

"In one more year I can take care of you," he says.

"I wouldn't burden you like that. You still have the chance to be someone."

Caleb shakes his head. "What's the point to any of it? I used to think that if I did my best I would be set for life. That I would have everything I need and that I would be happy. None of it matters if I can't have you."

"We have plenty of time to think about it. We're just kids..."

"No, we're not," Caleb says and takes my hand. "Old souls like ours are different. We don't spend a lifetime trying to figure out what makes us complete— we come back knowing exactly what does and set out to find it. This is all just one last test set before us."

I believe him, but I know the forces working against us are a hundred times stronger. "After four foster homes, I'm not passing any test soon," I reply.

"That's because you were never supposed to do it alone," Caleb says and rests his chin on my head. "Neither of us were."

He knew he had power over me, and I couldn't help but wonder if I held any over him in turn. "You don't know what it's like, to worry every moment of every day. Worry that something you did will break the glass under you and send you falling through. To not know if your mother will ever be able to take care of you again. To not know if your friends won't answer the phone because you're now a 'to avoid,' or because they've forgotten you. It's like nothing I see or touch anymore is real."

"Do you feel that way about me too?" Caleb asks with a solemn voice.

"No," I answer. "You're the only thing that is real to me, and maybe this place as well. But that only makes it all the easier for them to take it away." I get to my feet, not wanting to start crying in front of him.

He springs up and puts his palm against the tree behind me, pinning me in place. We look at each other for a while, searching each other's eyes for something. Maybe Caleb was right, and we were both old souls locked in a circle of suffering. Maybe we are doomed to always search for the one thing we can't have forever. Who was I to say otherwise? It was a sad thought, to think that all of this was some cruel joke by a higher power. One who laughed at you instead of answering your prayers.

He touches the side of my face with his other hand, and I smile, forcing the last of my remaining tears back into me. "I think we should get back before the cops come looking for me."

Caleb hesitates before nodding and letting me go. Then he puts his hands back into his blue jean pockets and starts back towards the house.

I lean against the tree for a few moments longer, where his touch has sent a chill up my spine, freezing me to the trunk. Once upon a time, I would have taken such a quiet moment to pray to return home. Only at that moment, I wasn't so sure. I could see what Caleb was trying to say, even though he didn't come right out with it. How could he? I could be shipped away tomorrow and never see him again. Shattering our hearts into pieces wouldn't accomplish anything but more pain. I was so tired of feeling hurt. I didn't know what would hit the weak spot of my glass heart and shatter the remains of my hope into dust.

I shake my head and force the negative thoughts away as I followed after him. I would cross that bridge when I got there. Until my mother got her drinking under control, I wouldn't be going home. And for the first time in two years, I was okay with that.

✿ ✿ ✿

I'm half awake when I hear two newly-familiar men talking with each other. My name is said, and it causes me to sit up. This time I'm on the leather sofa.

"Aubree, how did you get that bruise?" the newer man asks.

Which one? My whole head hurts now, and it's

impossible to guess how I landed.

"This one," he answers my thoughts and sets two fingers on the side of my eye.

His touch is so familiar that I go stiff. I remember this touch. I burn up like a kettle left too long on the stove. "I fell, chasing him," I lie, looking at Noah, who's sitting in the leather chair across from me. Pieces of his face are still in lying mode, and I figure that he had lied too. He could have only thought that I would be too ashamed to say anything about the truth of how pathetic my life is.

"See?" Noah says, lifting his hand in my direction. "I stole her wallet to confirm who she was, and she fell while chasing me."

The blond man lifts an eyebrow, unconvinced. "If that's true, then where were you taking her just now?"

"A friend's house," I answer for Noah. "Which I should be getting to before it gets too late — "

"It's two in the morning," the blond man replies. "We can take you there when you've had some rest. Unless you want to stay here longer?"

My face is back to melting point again. With the attention of two gorgeous men on me, I feel as if I won Goddess status. Even if one of them might be a demon.

"No, Caleb, she can't stay here. We don't have an extra bedroom, and the place is too small," Noah argues.

Caleb. I look closer at Caleb as he looks back my way.

His eyes grow mischievously wider as he knows what I'm thinking now. "I knew you would remember me. It's been a long time, Aubree."

Holy shit. He's real, and he's right next to me. My heart falls to the floor and rolls out of my reach. "How is it you? Where have you been all this time?"

"It's a long story, and it sounds like you have an equally long one. The short of it though is that shortly after I was transferred to another foster home, I got adopted. That loser over there who lacks the ability to pick up a girl in a normal fashion is my brother."

"You ungrateful ass," Noah replies, with his confident look returned. "I wasn't trying to pick her up. And you should be glad that I didn't convince our parents to leave your mutt-face in the window."

I'm suddenly watching night and day fight it out for dominance over the room. It's amusing, to say the least, and I can't help but smile. I reach into my pocket where something bulges. I pull out my small change purse and open it. There are several large bills inside. I close it too fast, as if there's a tarantula within. I dare to look at Noah now as he has his lying look at the ready again and it starts to make sense. He found me alright, but clearly, I was not who he had intended for his brother to see. The cash could have only been his inconspicuous way of telling me to get and stay lost.

"You alright?" Caleb asks as he focuses his attention back on me.

"I'm fine. Just tired. It's been the craziest day of my life, officially."

"That makes you the worst lightweight I've ever known," Caleb replies. He opens up the chest that doubles as the coffee table, pulling out a blanket and a pillow. He tucks me in on the couch, and I don't put up a fight. He's done this for me before, in what seems ages ago when I had a fever. I'm overflowing with nostalgia at this point.

"Goodnight, Aubree," Caleb says. "We will talk more after you had some rest."

"Night," I reply, too scared to say his name aloud lest everything around me vanishes into smoke before I close my eyes. I'll take in all of my fairy tale night away from home that I can. Tomorrow, I can go back to my sad reality. There, I can spend the rest of my life convincing myself that none of this ever happened, except in some impossible dream.

FIVE

Then

Along with my completely unplanned for sleepover, I get a dream that I haven't had for a long time. I'm watching a Springer Spaniel puppy as she hops about her siblings. The pup is determined to keep up. I give her the name Sapphire, even though she isn't mine. Every day I remember watching people come and go to the barn with one of her brothers or sisters, and every day I see her get left behind. All because her back legs work more like a rabbit's than a dog's. We're two broken puppies who are helpless to help each other, let alone ourselves. Our time together was running out, and with it, my ability to watch over and protect her.

My worker had called saying that the last meeting was coming up. It would be the one that would decide whether I continued to live here as a Crown Ward in foster care, or go home to my mother. My mom supposedly had her drinking under control, so it was looking good for my return. I head outside of the barn with Sapphire and throw the stick in my hand across the field. She takes off at full speed for it. If I had to bet on it, she could likely outrun a cheetah. It was when she walked back while gnawing on her stick that she had to hop a bit with her back legs. It didn't seem to bother her, and I wondered if ignorant bliss was the real happiness. Only humans were capable of passing cruel judgments on others.

I look over to the house on the hill, taking in one of the last days of summer as I sit in the grass. Sapphire lies down beside me and continues to gnaw on her stick. I had jinxed it then I realized, as I look to the end of the driveway to where my worker's car pulls in. What she wanted, I didn't know, but I mentally ran over in my head anything and everything that might call for trouble. I don't get up to greet her as she pulls up next to the barn and gets out of the car.

"What are you doing? We have to hurry, or we're going to be late!" she hollers.

I blink, not understanding what she was talking about. "The meeting isn't until the twenty-eighth," I countered.

"It's been moved up to today, didn't Lindsey tell you? Hurry and get ready and meet me back down here." At that, she gets back into her car and its air-conditioned coolness.

I look at my bare feet and then at Sapphire who has stopped chewing on her stick. I pick her up before my anxiety can paralyze me. I first head back to the barn to return her. Then I head up towards the house, but no amount of effort on my part will make my feet move any faster. I look around for Caleb before remembering that he and Lindsey had went into town earlier and her truck wasn't back yet. I couldn't do this now. I couldn't do this alone.

An impatient beep goes out from my worker's car, and I head into the house to put on my shoes, then back down to the barn. I wasn't going to get dressed pretty for my trial. I get into the back of my worker's car, and we start for the city. As usual, it's conversation-free. My worker doesn't appreciate my company any more than I do hers.

An hour and a half later, we reach the Children's Aid building, and I get out of the car. I wasn't ready for this, but then again it wouldn't matter if I were. Whatever they would decide was what was going to happen. I would just be a silent witness to the sentencing of my own life.

I wiped the feeling-sorry-for-myself look off of my face and followed my worker. This was my fifth one, and I could only imagine how much trouble I was to have to be handed off to different ones so many times. We reach the large meeting room, and I find a variety of people I have never seen before in my life. At the center of the chairs at the table sits my mom, overwhelmed by them all. She looks worse than me. I can't begin to imagine how much medication she had to down to make it here. The endless scrutiny of being an unfit mother looms over every inch of her. I sit down next to her, and we talk for a while. She's distant; as if her body is here, but her mind is miles away.

After a few minutes, the last of the jury comes in, and the meeting starts. As it progresses, so does my hate for these people. Why were they doing this to us? How had the problem of my mother's drinking turned into the topic of her medication and the rough area we lived in? When my friends from my old life were brought into question, I couldn't take it anymore, and I kicked my chair back with my legs. I wanted to scream. I wanted to tell all of these people to go straight to Hell. I wanted to run away and get lost somewhere where they would never find me. None of these words escaped me. Our life was being put on trial with a sentence of permanent separation. Despite that, I couldn't so much as muster enough courage together to storm out of the room.

There was no light or any kind of hope here. My mother and I were hopelessly outnumbered. I could see now that there was never a chance of going home. It was a stacked game from the start, and that infuriated me even more. It was never about what was best for me — but what was best according to their rule book.

"Aubree, come into the next room with me for a moment."

I look at the director, and I imagine punching the smart-ass glasses off of his face. I didn't want to talk to him — I wanted out of this place before I did something irreversibly stupid that I might or might not regret.

He calls me again, and I go into the little office. I watch him sit down in the desk chair as I close the door behind me. I didn't hear anything he said. It was more crap about my mother being unfit and ridiculous things unheard of until now. I would not give up my friends and my home for anyone. I didn't give a damn that my life wasn't good enough for him — I wanted it back.

"What is it that you want?"

I wasn't sure I was hearing him straight when he asks me this. "You're asking me now what I want after shuffling me from one godforsaken foster home to the next? Why the hell should I think what I ever wanted mattered to you in the least? A violent outbreak in my first home, move me to another. A jealous foster mother, then an assault from a foster kid who belongs in a cage, just move me again and again. At just what point do I snap and go crazy? And never once did you ask or give a shit about what I wanted. Now suddenly it's all about what I want? Because you people have no clue how to do your job properly?" None of my emergency brakes were working, and I didn't care. If the whole building came crumbling down the next moment, I wouldn't have stopped to care. All I knew was that my mother was crying in the other room and that with or without me, we had to get out of here before we both exploded.

The supervisor had heard enough, and got up and opened the door back into the room. I stormed in and then right out of the meeting room, having had enough group therapy for a lifetime.

The smell of blood pulls me into another time and place, and I look around to find myself in the woods behind my foster home. I look down at my hands to find that my knuckles are bleeding. Even more terrifyingly, I'm backed against a tree with a pack of wolves before me. The growls and snaps from the wolves' teeth threaten to tear me to pieces at any moment. I watch their demon-like, dilated eyes in a frozen horror. They can only want me dead. I hear Caleb's voice call out my name, and I yell at him to get away. I don't know whether the wolves were ever real, or just a vivid demon.

"Aubree!"

I turn to look where Caleb appears from the trees and then I quickly look back to where the wolves once were. Only there's no sign that they were ever so much as there.

"You scared the life out of me. Did something attack you?" Caleb asks as he approaches.

Time is wrong in this nightmare. The wolves didn't come for me until my knight had moved foster homes and left me by myself. I didn't want to lose Caleb. Yet I had no power to keep him from being taken from me. I bring my thoughts back into focus and try to calculate the time. "What time is it?"

"Noon about now." He's pulling me back to the house, and we head up to the kitchen. I'm despondent. "So what happened?" he asks again.

"I messed up. I completely freaked out on the director. I was so mad that I barely remember half of it."

"What did he say?" Caleb asks in concern.

"There was this whole room of people. Somehow, overnight, the topic of my mother and her drinking expanded to where I lived, my friends... They just picked off everything like it all wasn't a match for their 'perfect' ideals. It was horrible. When he took me into the next room to talk to me alone, I just went completely ape-shit on him."

"I'm sorry that I wasn't there for you when you needed me the most." Caleb is kneeling next to my knee now as if it was somehow his fault. "No one said that the meeting was today."

"My worker probably did it on purpose. It's easier to convict someone in a trial if they have no time to assemble a defense."

"Well, I don't care what they say. I'm still keeping you forever," Caleb assures me.

I smile as his warm glow makes it impossible not to.

His puppy eyes break me every time. I can't stay mad or crazy around him for long. He takes my hand and kisses it. It's only then that I realize my hand is covered in blood and I pull it away.

"How long until they come to a decision?" Caleb asks.

I dart my gaze back at him. I'm unsure if he can see the same blood on me that I can. "I don't know. Maybe a week?"

It's not the answer he wants when he catches my face in his hands and kisses me. It catches me by surprise, but I find myself kissing him back. After a short stop in time, he pulls away and leaves me in a complete daze.

"That was supposed to come after your birthday present," he says with a smile.

"Birthday?" I ask. Then it hits — today is my birthday. Even my own mother didn't seem to remember, let alone me. Count on the most perfect boy in the universe to remember it for me.

"Don't tell me you forgot?" Caleb asks.

I shake my head to try and substantiate the lie. Judging from his expression, it's not working. He sees through me too easy. I'm fifteen now. One year away from possible freedom. If I don't break completely by then. Caleb hands me the little pink box, and I open it. Inside, a small figurine of a knight in shining armor stands at guard, staring back at me with a sword in hand. I giggle and realize that he was right all along— my fantasy monster toy collection was missing a heroic rescuer. This one looks to be solid pewter.

"Do you like it?" he asks.

"Do I have to choose between this one and my real-life version?" I ask.

"It's a package deal," he assures me.

I smile and kiss him on my own accord this time, before hugging him tightly. He holds onto me, and I feel safe from everything. I dare a glance at my hands and see that the blood has vanished like a bad dream. If only the force of time wasn't as heartless as it is.

SIX

Now

In the morning, my dream vacation is over. A gentle touch from Caleb's hand on my arm wakes me back up to reality.

"Morning sleeping beauty. Any nice dreams?"

"Yes, and some evil person is trying to wake me up from one," I grumble and turn around, hiding my face in the couch.

"You can't sleep all day. Now get up and get ready. I'm taking you out for breakfast. Let me know if these fit, too."

"Fit?" I ask aloud and sit up as I try to force myself out of my sleepy haze. Sure enough, there is a pair of blue jeans and a white blouse with a light floral print on the leather chair. "You keep women's clothes?"

"Of course. Noah likes to wear them whenever he can," Caleb jokes as he pours himself a glass of milk in the kitchen.

I look at him with one eyebrow raised.

"Okay, okay, fine. Noah's a fashion designer."

"Even worse— how in blazes did he find anything that fits me? I'm like a size nine and then some. He must have had an emergency elephant closet."

Caleb laughs and almost loses his milk. "He wasn't too keen on the challenge, but he never backs down from a dare. That and you aren't fat— his anorexic women are by far less appealing."

I lift the brand new garments up with a smile I can't contain. Designer clothing. This is a first for me.

"Hurry up with your shower, or we're going to miss the morning menu. You'll find everything you need in there. I'm going to warm up the car."

I'm on my feet as instructed, but I find myself looking around instead. "Where's Noah?"

"Work," Caleb replies as he swings on his jean jacket and heads out the door.

I bundle up the clothes in my arms and hustle into the washroom. My million questions can wait until I look like a human member of society again. I set a new record for fastest shower ever and get dressed. Most of my time is used looking in the mirror and making sure that my hair is covering my bruise. I hear the front door open, and I come out of the washroom just as Caleb returns for me. He smiles, and I give myself another quick look over. "You have to thank your brother for me — he got it all spot on."

"Good. Cause if he got anything wrong, he will be finding another model for his spring campaign," Caleb replies.

"You model for him? Sounds like fun." He's a model? Holy crap I'm out of my league. I was out of my league ten years ago. I'm even more out of it now. Despite that sad fact, I'm happy that one of us made it out of foster care to become a normal, happy person. If not almost famous.

"Let's go," he says and heads out again.

I follow him out of the apartment and downstairs, towards the car. I feel like I'm walking into a trap now. Only a conversation could arise over breakfast together. I'm left with less than minutes to invent my more acceptable and easier to chew persona as I get into the car. It takes me a moment to realize how much more relaxed I am around Caleb than I was with Noah despite it all. "Where we headed?"

"It's a surprise. That and I do believe you will like it."

"Alright," I say as we pull out of the underground parking lot. A short drive through the city later, and we pull into a Golden Griddle. I laugh as the secret is up.

"I remember you mentioning that your mother promised to take you here for years. So just in case she never did, I've taken it on myself to make sure you taste these pancakes."

I'm giggling now like I used to when I was younger. I have no counter-argument. Pancakes need none. "She never did get around to it." I follow Caleb inside, and we take up a seat next to the window. There are only a few people around, and I don't feel overwhelmed.

Caleb orders a stack of pancakes for both of us and then turns his entire focus on me. "Ten years. I still can't get over it. I'm amazed that you recognized me," Caleb says.

"You really thought I would forget you that easily?" I reply.

"To think that I even had a picture to help me out. Did you keep yours?" Caleb asks.

I remember the day we took the picture he speaks of like it was yesterday. It was when I met Caleb for the first time, at his birthday party that our foster mother held for him. And I remember the picture to its last detail where we all sat squished together on the hay-loaded trailer. Even more clearly do I remember the first moment I lay eyes on him, from the other side of that trailer. He was the most handsome boy I had ever seen. It was as if he wore his perfect soul around him like a visible aura that just made him glow. It was one of my happiest days. I had never thought that falling instantly in love with someone was possible until then. "Most of my things were lost in the moves."

"I can't begin to imagine what you went through since I left. I tried everything I could to find you, but it was as if you vanished into thin air."

More like a tiny apartment, locked away from the world, but close enough, I think to myself. My excuses for hiding away from the world are too pathetic for this conversation.

"Where did they put you?" Caleb asks.

"Shortly after you left, they moved me to a boy's foster home."

"What? How can they do that?" Caleb asks in disbelief.

"Supposedly they had nowhere else to put me." I don't mention the wolves that may or may not have happened.

"But that was only for a while, right? You went home to your mother?"

"Yes, about two weeks later." I didn't mention all the other details as to why, or what had happened in those two weeks.

"Did things work out?" he asks as he takes the coffee that the server hands him and passes mine over first.

I load up the cup with sugar and bit of milk. I'm not sure where to start in the direction of my lying now.

"Aubree," Caleb says and puts his hand on top of mine.

"Sorry, I drifted off for a sec there. It was fine between her and me. For a few months, anyways."

Caleb's face looks hurt now, and I feel like kicking myself. "I had found your mother's place, but by the time I did, she said you weren't living there anymore. Where did you go?"

I didn't think ahead to the possibility of him doing something like that. He said he would, but it sounded too impossible at the time for me to accept as a very real possibility. I didn't think anyone gave a damn about me back then and that I was fortunate that Phil was interested in me. Suddenly my story was a giant knot of a mess in my head. "I ran away, and couch surfed from my friends' houses pretty much after that." Another lie. I was dying inside a bit more after every one.

"What about now? Noah says you have your own place up on Hester Street?"

"Yeah," I say, and almost stab my pancakes with the painful thought of having to go home. "I'm pretty solid now."

"You ever take up that writer's life that you wanted?" Caleb asks.

I think of the mess of handwritten papers of novels I have written at home. Phil likely burned them all now just to spite me. "Yeah, but I'm still too scared to show them to anyone."

Caleb smiles and finishes chewing his bite of pancakes. "If that's the case, then I absolutely insist on being the first one to read the next bestselling author."

I almost choke on my food. "I don't think I'm anywhere close to being that just yet. But I'll keep you updated." He's trying so hard to keep my spirits high, even though my heart feels like it has an anvil tied to it.

Caleb tells his story then, and how he went to one other foster home before being picked for adoption. I still remember the day I woke up to find him no longer there. I had nearly lost my mind in grief. But now, Caleb's story plays out like a happy Hollywood flick in my head.

"I can just imagine Noah standing there, sizing you up for his future plans. And you looking totally lost as to just what he wants from you."

"You're not too far from the truth of what happened." Caleb laughs. "Noah is definitely my opposite in like...every sense. He can be downright terrifying at times. But he's been the best brother I could have ever asked for."

I finish my pancakes before him and watch as the server takes away my empty, syrup-sticky plate. "He looks like he's used to getting what he wants."

"He's sorry about that fall you had chasing him, too. He's not very good at giving apologies in person."

One hell of a fall, I think to myself. "I've already forgotten it. Being spoiled for a whole day will do that."

"Well, I've only started with you. Tomorrow, you're coming out to dinner with me," Caleb says.

I can feel my face go a bit pale at the idea of trying to sneak out of the apartment a second time. I might not so much as survive sneaking back in the minute Phil sees me.

"Aubree?"

"Sorry, I just need the washroom real quick." I get up and make my way to the restroom and lock myself in a stall. I need to reset. I'm doing the exact opposite of what I had planned. Noah has already made it clear that he wants me to disappear. I have already convinced myself that Caleb is way out of my league. Even if he weren't, the psychopath I have at home would quickly dismantle the slightest breeze of happiness to whisper its way into my life. I take in a deep breath and leave the washroom.

Caleb is waiting patiently when I get back. "You ready to get going?"

"Yeah, sorry about that. Just had a bit of a sugar rush

get to my head."

"That sounds like you. It's amazing that you don't have diabetes with the amount of sugar you put in your coffee. There isn't that much sugar in my place in a month."

I laugh as I imagine just that.

Caleb drives me home, and I turn to thank him but find that he's distracted by something else and doesn't unlock the door.

"This is your building?"

I look out the window to confirm just that. The rundown building fits perfectly on the street where several gangs hang out. One is sitting next to the graffiti-covered walls. This would be the definition of a hard sell to the high-class club that Caleb is now part of. "Yeah. It's fortunately not as bad as it looks, don't worry."

"I am now officially and irreversibly worried about you. I don't even want to imagine what the apartments look like in here, let alone the tenants..." Caleb says in concern.

I tug at the lock on my door. It won't budge. "I'll be fine."

"Dinner, tomorrow at five. I'm kidnapping you if I have to," Caleb warns.

"Alright. I promise." I lie.

Caleb nods and opens the locks with a push of a button from his side.

"Thank you for everything. I never thought that having my wallet stolen and a bump on my head could be such a good thing. I had a lot of fun."

"Don't mention it. Not at least until I have the chance to kill Noah, officially."

I smile and open the door, before closing it behind me and waving him off. I turn around and look up at the balconies to my rundown building. I feel relieved to have protected my one perfect memory from the reality of what is my life. Even if I still feel sadder than I ever have with the thought that I will likely never see him again.

SEVEN

Now

I slowly open the door to my apartment, fearing the fist that might come for me if I'm caught. I can see the TV giving the room a flickering glow, and I come all the way inside. I know I'm crazy for returning. Clearly, I have a death-wish. But there are a few things I need to take with me if I am to run; should I gather the courage to face the streets alone. But now I have money. It's not enough to get an apartment of my own, but it's enough to eat for a bunch of days.

I close the door and look at the couch to where no one sits. I don't see Phil anywhere. I touch my jean pocket with my wallet inside. I go into the kitchen and fill a glass with tap water, before drinking the whole thing. I breathe in deeply as I leave the kitchen and head to my tiny bed. I'm determined to just sleep the rest of forever away with my last perfect memory. I curl up and thank God for it, as he did answer my wish, even though he usually only answers prayers out of necessity. He answered me, and I wasn't ready. I had assumed that anyone who might give the slightest care about me would be near my level. Caleb had ascended to a much higher status quo above me, completely and totally out of my reach. I close my eyes and let sleep take me away from my new sad reality.

When I wake up, I can feel someone touching me. I let my brain catch up to me from the deepness of sleep. Now I can confirm that someone has their hand near my pocket. I open my eyes and see that it's Phil. Usually, I would scream at him at this point to stop groping me. Yet this time I know he's after something more valuable in his eyes than my pride; my freedom that is contained in my wallet. I sit up, and he takes his hand away from me. "What do you want?"

"Where were you?" he asks in his usual demanding fashion.

"Taking a very long walk."

Phil gets to his feet, and I can tell he's sober as his brown eyes are all here. His stance is about as straight as it gets for him.

Suddenly his sober mood is causing the hairs on my arm to rise in fear when usually it's only his drunken mode that terrifies me the most. He walks over to the closet and pulls out what looks like my ancient knapsack from when I was in high school. What he has planned doesn't click in until he throws it at my feet.

"Get out."

I pick up the bag and keep one eye on him as I look inside. The few articles of clothing that I own are crumpled within. And my writings. So he didn't throw them in the trash.

"I said get out!"

Technically he can throw me out. We are just really hateful roommates. I never had the chance to keep a job that he didn't burn into oblivion from under my feet. I'm no good for sex anymore, as he is clearly tired of having to force and threaten it out of me. I'm nothing and no one. This was part of my original plan; to run away from this state of being nothing. I was cowering out of the plan, and now it's being forced on me. Somehow it seems so much easier this way. I pick up the bag and head out the door. I never so much as think about looking back.

❊ ❊ ❊

I find my way downtown, and after asking around, I stumble on a homeless shelter. The small building isn't anything special on the outside. It doesn't so much as have a sign. If it weren't for the really, really long line outside, I would think that I have the wrong place.

"What are you doing?"

The familiar voice scares the wits out of me, and I jump in fright. I turn around and find Noah standing there, looking completely out of place in a sharp black jacket and white shirt. He looks like he just finished attending a fancy dinner.

"Why are you still stalking me?" I ask. I can't think of any other reason that he might be here.

"I can't seem to be able to leave you alone for a minute. Every time I turn around, you're getting beaten up or lining up at a homeless shelter."

"Well, I didn't choose either," I reply.

"So he threw you out? You know there's laws that— ?"

"Yeah, for normal people," I say, cutting Noah off. "I have never paid a cent of rent or for food other than for my sugar cravings with what change would fall out of the laundry. I never could. The cops would just as quickly haul my ass out."

"Unless you locked him up for assault," Noah adds.

"Where he then gets out and is angry enough to kill me for real. No thanks."

"Then why didn't you have Caleb drive you to your friend's house like you said you were going to?" Noah asks.

"Look, Noah, I get it okay?" I say, changing the subject. "You're worried that somehow I'm going to wiggle my way back into yours and Caleb's perfect life. I can assure you that it won't happen. I know when I'm out of my league, and when to get out of the way."

"Well since that's clear," Noah says as if relieved to have finally gotten to the point he was waiting for in the conversation, "best of luck getting a bed tonight." He turns then and starts to leave.

"Wait!" I call after him.

Noah stops and looks back at me.

"I just need to know why you started all this? Why go through all the effort of finding me for Caleb only to want me to disappear just as quickly?"

Noah takes a couple of steps back towards me, his hands locked behind him. "Just recently our parents dropped us with an ultimatum for at least one of us to find a woman and settle down. If we don't, we will be cut off from the financial hive. Unfortunately, I can't be much use in stopping that from happening. I don't take any interest in women aside from putting clothes on them. The unfortunate timing of it all also happens to make my career very dependent on our parent's support. That aside, finding a proper woman for Caleb has been tough. Heck, it has been downright impossible. I couldn't figure out the whys to it all until I stumbled on his diary. It turns out that he never moved on from his puppy affection towards you."

I feel a large lump build up in my throat. It won't go down, as the idea that Caleb has thought about me for so long just doesn't compute. "Sorry that I'm not the wealthy Duchess you were hoping for."

"Money doesn't have a lot to do with it," Noah continues. "Any woman who were to meet our parents would have an instant background check, a status quo check, and at the very least need a job. You would be instantly shredded. I've already caused you enough misfortune to so much as think about exposing you to that kind of ridicule. The lifestyles of the rich and famous kills souls and leaves nothing but their husks behind, masquerading around in boredom. You wouldn't fit in."

I'm surprised at his play at poetry. He almost makes his world sound worse than mine. "So what will you tell Caleb? That I just vanished off the map?"

"Exactly. Because that's what needs to happen," Noah states flatly.

His tone is so cold; it sends a shiver through me. I nod as I finally get the lump in my throat down. "Okay then. Thanks for the money. I will pay you back when I can."

"Don't worry about it."

I lift the strap from my knapsack higher onto my

shoulder and get in line with the rest of the bottom-dwellers of society. When I look back to where Noah had been standing, he's gone.

EIGHT

Now

I haven't been this cold for a very, very long time. Not since I decided to try and run away at my last foster home. Every part of my body had felt as frozen then as it does now. I was hungry, thirsty, and too miserable and lost in depression to care if I lived or died. It had all fallen through back then. The glass under my feet had shattered. Caleb was gone again, and once again I was alone.

Except for the wolves that had attacked me when I was still in foster care. A part of me wanted them to tear me apart now, piece by piece so that I didn't have to feel the pain in my heart anymore. The wolves that had attacked me had also made me one of them. It was enough to help me escape the system and its need to make me into some docile pet. From what I figured, they didn't want a death on their hands. Now things were different. I was in control of my life, and there was nothing and no one out here who would ever push my life in their intended direction again. Freedom was a great idea. Surviving it was now another story.

I woke up with a start and found myself on the park bench I had fallen asleep on, with my knapsack tucked under my head.

"Hey, get up. You can't sleep here."

My ears and eyes are too frozen to know if it's Noah taunting me or not, so I looked up. An older police officer is staring angrily back down at me. I guess freedom from the system wasn't going to happen anytime soon, either.

"Did you hear me?"

I pick up my knapsack and swing it over my shoulder, as I will my feet and legs to unfreeze. Satisfied that I won't topple over, I get up and start walking. I don't know where to go, so I just walk. I hope that fate has some clue as to what it is doing with me. I don't get far, as exhaustion and the cold finally win, and I collapse in the park.

❊ ❊ ❊

I don't know how long I'm out for when I wake up and feel like my entire body is on fire. I sense someone staring at me, and I turn my head to the side to see Caleb sitting next to me in his car. I wish he would say something, as the silence causes this ringing in my ears that won't shut up.

"How are you feeling?" he asks.

Like absolute shit. "How did I get here?"

"You missed our dinner date. So I went up to your apartment, after having to ask several neighbors who have never met you despite being on your floor. Then I got to meet your husband, who also had no idea of where you disappeared to."

I feel like throwing up. "My husband? Oh hell no." I'm laughing now as the madness of it all is just too much to keep inside.

"You could have just told me that you're — "

"I'm not married!" I scream at him. It's not the way I want it to come out. "Sorry," I say and take in a deep breath to calm myself down.

"So that's why you vanished for ten years. What were you? His girlfriend?" Caleb asks, his face now turned to that of serious concern.

"A coward too scared to do something to escape to a better life. How did you find me?" I ask, fearing that I might have gotten Caleb into trouble somehow.

"Finding you in the woods is what I've always been

good at. What are you doing Aubree? Did you think that I wouldn't help you? You could have froze to death!"

"I'm not your responsibility," I reply, trying to stay calm.

"What if I want you to be my responsibility?"

"Noah has already made it clear that he doesn't want me around. I'm nobody, and I don't want to come between you and your brother."

"So that's what this is about..." Caleb says as he keeps his focus on the road. "You're not coming between us, silly."

I drop the side of my head against the window before the bruise there surges me back with pain. Caleb shakes his head and looks at me briefly before looking back at the road.

"That creep back at your apartment did that, didn't he?"

I don't answer.

"I'm going to kill him and then — " Caleb says.

"No, you aren't," I interrupt him. "You can't kill Noah for wanting to protect you."

"Protect me from who? You? Aubree, you ever stop to think that you aren't alone in the world? That there are those who care about you?"

Never crossed my mind. But I don't say it aloud. I rest the back of my head against the seat. It's then that I get a cold chill down my spine and I sit back up, before looking to the back seat of the car. Noah is sitting there, quieter than a ghost. This bastard just won't leave me alone.

Caleb looks in the rear-view mirror with a scowl on his face.

I feel incredibly awkward and sink further into my seat.

"So I took the liberty of reading through all her medical history earlier," Noah says to Caleb. He is purposely leaving me out of the conversation as I did him. Only I didn't do it on purpose. "Turns out my newest friend here once got attack by a pack of six wolves and beat them off. Then she dragged her bleeding self out of the woods on her own for help. Pretty impressive."

"Is that true?" Caleb asks, taking his eyes off the road momentarily to look at me.

I don't answer.

"Where was this? Back at the foster home?" Caleb asks.

"It doesn't matter anymore," I say, trying not to sound bitter.

"It could have only happened after I left. Jesus," Caleb curses.

"Well, whatever happened, you've completely changed my initial judgment of you Aubree," Noah says. He's back to his teasing voice.

"Oh?" I ask.

"I've met a lot of people in my life, but never one who has survived a pack of wolves. Because of that, I think you will fit into our life just fine."

Caleb is looking with a frown in the rear-view mirror again when Noah leans back. "The only difference being that the wolves in high society sports sheep's clothing."

"Designer clothing, thank you very much," Noah rebukes.

I let out a long sigh as I'm too weak to fight this battle. I close my eyes and remember the wolves that I had shoved into the back of my memory for so long as something that never happened. I feel like I'm kicking and screaming at them all over again, until they finally give up and flee, leaving me to bleed my way out of the woods on my own. I was right back there all over again.

NINE

Now

My first test for entry into high society arrives two days later. I'm thoroughly spoiled by the attention that Caleb gives me by this point. I wake up on the couch and smell the pancakes in the kitchen. Damn Noah for being the only one who can cook so well. He is the uncontested Master of the kitchen, where no mere mortal may enter. I have no idea how to bite the hand that feeds me and still get food. I sit up against my body's need to go back to sleep and look at the window as sunlight starts to fill it in.

"Before you even think of running into this kitchen for your pancakes, look down," Noah says.

I've already learned that arguing with Noah usually ends up with me starving, so I comply. I look down at the fluffy white carpet. There is a pair of silver, high-heeled shoes on them.

"Put them on and come get your pancakes."

"That's it? No balancing books for my head to go with it?" I ask.

"That's for tomorrow."

I could swear I see him smile, but he's fast about it. Way to go my fat mouth. I grumble and look at the shoes. Doesn't seem too hard. I slip them on and carefully get to my feet. The soft carpet is making the simple task of walking in heels precariously dangerous. I focus on the prize and start for the kitchen. I only get halfway before my right ankle twists under me, and my ass collides with the floor.

Noah lifts an eyebrow, unimpressed. Instead of helping me, he taunts me further by loudly putting a bottle of syrup next to my plate of pancakes, as if to sweeten the deal.

Sugar calls to me through the pain and I clumsily get to my feet, even though I'm about as balanced as a drunk. I inch closer to the counter and sit down on the high bar stool, then reach for my food. I start to devour it like it's my last meal.

"When was the last time you walked in heels?" Noah asks.

I think about it, but I can't remember. "Been a while."

Noah checks my face for any sign of lying, before opening a bottle of Perrier water. "I swear you were born yesterday or something. Didn't you ever go out? Hit the clubs? Leave your apartment?" He finishes with a laugh.

I find none of it very funny, so I put more syrup on my pancakes to spite him. "You already witnessed what happens to me when I leave my former apartment." It comes out colder than I intended.

Noah loses the smile on his face and looks around for a change of topic. He goes over to his leather jacket and drops my next homework on the counter as I finish the last of my pancakes off. He takes my plate away and pushes the file to me.

I open it and find a bunch of pictures of models inside. They're thin enough to fit several into my skin. "What's this?"

"The outfits that I have lined up for Saturday's show. What do you think of them?"

Feeling my chance to strike his ego back, I shuffle through them. "Horrible. Too pale. This looks like a fatty extension of her skin. This one is okay. So is this one. This one needs to be burned...like immediately."

Noah nods and seems to approve of my judgments. "Thanks." He takes the pictures back and puts them into the file. He comes around the bar and takes my heels off, one after the other.

I blush even though it's wasted on him. "So what's next, Boss? Jumping through hoops of fire?"

"Today we teach you how to survive." He disappears into the bedroom for a moment. He emerges with a white and pink floral dress way over my pay grade. Apparently, he has some obsession with dressing me in floral prints.

"That sounds....fun," I complain. "Please tell me it's fire."

"Nope. I'm going to take you out for a test run past my parents."

I turn cold. "Wait— wasn't I suppose to be Caleb's girlfriend and your meal-ticket? Or did I get that backward?"

"Nope. But this way it will be easier to make adjustments, should my parents decide to tear you into tiny little pieces. Caleb's too soft."

And Noah is too evil. He hands me the dress, and I fear it's what I'll be wearing in my coffin. He goes into the closet near the front door then and pulls me out a pair of matching flat shoes. "Hurry up. We don't want to be late."

I comply, and head into the washroom to get dressed. He gives me the precise amount of time that I need to get the dress on, before unlocking the bathroom from outside and pulling me out. I feel like a doll being led around as he sits me down on the armrest of the leather chair. He expertly starts to pull my hair into an elaborate braid before tying it off. I hate him, but the man knows how to dress his dolls. He has my makeup on before I can get fidgety and we're out the door.

We end up driving to what looks like a high-end department store, and he makes it clear that I'm not to wander off on my own. I figure that he has timed his parent's shopping habits to this place and that any moment will be my last. The trap seems simple enough, but something feels off. Aside from me being very, very far from Walmart. Before I can ponder making a run for it, Noah has my hand locked in his, and I'm looking at two new people who he greets.

"Mom, Dad, this is Aubree who I told you about. Aubree, these are my parents," Noah says.

"Oh my, she's so pretty," the older woman replies and looks at her husband. There is a similar look of approval on his face.

"Mr. and Mrs. McCowan," I say, quickly straightening up. "It's an honor to meet you both finally." I'm shocked by how quickly I've adjusted to the situation.

"The honor is all ours," Mr. McCowan says and shakes my hand.

"I thought I'd make it a double surprise for Aubree today," Noah says with his flawless charm.

I keep my smile up as I ponder over just what Noah is talking about.

"Ah yes, you mentioned that you would take her shopping for a ring today. By the heavens, if that's the case, I won't have my son buy anything from here. I insist that you let me call the store where I bought your mother's ring downtown. They have such better quality," Mr. McCowan says.

My veins are turning into ice, and I look at Noah who doesn't look back. He gives a firm grip of my hand in warning, instead.

"If you insist, Dad," Noah says and continues to talk with his parents.

I'm completely cornered, as there is nowhere to run without bringing the whole house of cards down around me.

"Well, I will catch you two lovebirds later," Mrs. McCowan says, snapping me out of my paralyzed state.

"Of course," I reply, and I watch as they both leave.

Noah tugs me out of the store and back towards the car, stuffing me into the passenger seat before going around to the driver's side.

"What the hell just happened?" I yell at him.

"Minor change of plans," he answers as he starts up the car.

"But you're gay — how is this supposed to work? Caleb is going to freak out! I'm seriously not doing this!"

"Relax, woman. This is only temporary until I get my money," Noah says, attempting to reassure me.

"You're a monster," I hiss back at him. "Have you never told your parents that you're — ?"

"What? Gay? No, of course not. How would your parents react to that kind of news?"

I don't have an answer to give him or a parent that ever gave a shit about me long enough to ask such a crazy question. "I never signed up to be your wife."

"Think of it this way," Noah says as he pulls out of the mall's parking lot. "You get to be a princess for a few months, and then you get your happily ever after with Caleb. Provided you learn how to behave."

"I still don't get why you're doing this…?"

"It's all about keeping up appearances. That, and you need a lot of work if you're going to fit in. The whole 'from the hood' act isn't going to work around my parents, particularly since Caleb is sporting enough of it as it is."

I sink into my seat, hiding my nails under my arms lest I scratch his eyes out.

"And you just let me worry about Caleb," Noah says as he briefly glances my way.

"This is all some sort of sick game to you, isn't it?"

"Sick, no. And if it were a game, it would be about

winning the money. Don't be such a sourpuss. How many girls get to have two attractive guys serving on them hand and foot, feeding and dressing them for three months? Try and enjoy yourself."

I look out the window as I try to take it all in. "If you try and kiss me — at any point for whatever reason — I will break your jaw, and this charade is over."

"Deal," Noah responds without hesitation. "Besides, you're not my type."

"No shit," I grumble and close my eyes. I wish I could sleep through the rest of the mess I've landed myself in this time. It's then when an idea pops into my head. "Noah, you think you can swing us past my mother's?"

"Uh, why?" he asks.

"Well, you just reminded me of how my mother always used to tell me that I would never amount to anyone, let alone get a decent guy. Yet here I am with the perfect guy..." I continue to mock him. "Besides, I met your parents, fiancée; now you have to meet mine."

"You can't be serious...?" Noah groans.

"Hey! What I'm asking for isn't difficult. Do it, or I'll be the one to pull the tablecloth out from under your little game with your parents."

Noah rolls his eyes back. "Do I want to know where I'm driving?"

I smile as revenge is now within my grasp.

TEN

Then

When I was still young enough to wear green outfits with white polka dots, I was also young enough to fall victim to my mother's scare tactic. I've yet to meet a parent who didn't have one of some sort, but my mother devised the best one ever created in the history of the Universe. She did this by combining my fear of the dark with her own 'black hole' theory. It was simple, but it worked. If you're a bad kid and didn't listen to your parents, then you got taken away and dropped into a dark room. This room was void of any light and all human contact. Eventually, I grew too old to fall for it anymore and easier to negotiate with on an intellectual level. That got my chores done without the threat of total oblivion. Little did I know that the Universe had already posed itself to turn on me despite this.

Whoever said you couldn't be poor and have a happy life apparently never lived as I did. I was surrounded by friends, and all the outdoor entertainment one could ask for. I had a mom who I took for granted in having all to myself and I was constantly busy. No one saw this girl as being poor or ever hungry, or unhappy in the slightest. I was better off than most of my peers in my building. One just had to look at the neighborhood to get a general idea of the area and its inhabitants. We were all poor. We were all with our problems that we were unable to solve ourselves, or just stuck on where society failed us. In one way or another, we were all the same.

Getting through school with straight A's and a positive character to boot, there was never a problem that I and my mom couldn't handle. Or one that I hadn't learned from an early age to avoid. Gangs? Drugs? Walk the other way. Sexual predators? Stick closer to your friends, who like you, watched the news last week of the girl who was caught alone. Building on fire for the second time in the same month and suffocating in smoke? That one was always a bit tricky, particularly since my mother would go into near-shock from being terrified of fire. Wild shootings and multiple victims? It's alright, I slept in, and that alone likely saved my life on more than one occasion. Every day I was grateful to God who despite the millions of problems plaguing my area, was still watching my back.

Then the money got too low. Diagnosed with Schizophrenia, my mother did what many disabled people in our area did; rely on the disability check from the government every month. When it was suddenly cut drastically, there would be nothing I could do to stop the impending disaster. As my mother's stress level rose with how hard it had become to put food on the table, I did what I could to avoid the home front and her drinking that made her volatile. Going out with my friends quickly became all-nighters where I didn't return until five in the morning. Going to school meant staying after school as long as possible and then finding something else to do outside of the house. Hours once used for homework and studying became non-existent. It was when my mother started drinking heavily that things exploded completely out of my control. Scared for my safety I ran, but I couldn't run far enough to escape the next day.

Now I was coming back to my childhood home with everything my mother said I would never have. It was all a lie, but I was curious to see how she would react. I doubted that I would be dealing out any I told you so's today. If anything, she would still find something that she could use to cut out the tiny bit of my remaining heart.

Noah wasn't getting out of the car, and I couldn't blame him as he looked up at the decrepit apartment building beside us. "You do have theft insurance, right?" I ask. I'm not joking.

Noah looks at me with a frown. "No way I'm going in there."

"Yep. You are."

"And if I refuse?" Noah replies.

"I take this 'hood' to a dinner with your parents later. I'm sure they'll be interested to hear about my upbringing. Then I'll go for the tablecloth." I'm threatening him, but it comes easily. I have nothing to lose but the illusionary cage he's thrown over my head.

Noah sighs with frustration as he opens the car door. I watch as he checks the car locks twice, and then he follows me inside. We reach the lobby and Noah looks to be feeling seriously out of place. The smell of weed fills the area, and a rowdy bunch of teenagers brushes past us as they leave the elevator. Once we are inside and heading upstairs, he covers his nose from the smell of urine. But he quietly soldiers on and is relieved when we get out of the elevator, only to be grossed out again when a cockroach skitters past.

"Good god, this place is unbelievably disgusting. You seriously lived here?"

"For fifteen years. Now, there is also another thing you have to know about my mother."

Noah takes a moment to adjust before looking at me.

"She is really, really critical about details. So no bad news. No bad anything, and mind your tone."

"Okay," Noah says.

"And whatever you do, don't comment on her place or sit down anywhere."

"Why can't we sit?" Noah asks, confused.

"Unless you want bedbugs biting at you tonight, just stay standing."

Noah's face is paler now as he silently gulps and follows me to the apartment at the end of the hall. "Those are real?"

I take in a deep breath and give the secret knock. It takes a few times, but my mother answers and I can hear her slippers shuffle on the other side of the door.

She opens it and looks first at me, before looking at Noah. "Well well, you finally come and visit. Who's this?" my mother asks, not intimidated by Noah's towering presence.

"Mom, this is Noah, my fiancée."

"Hello," Noah says in greeting, but it's not well received.

My mom laughs briefly and then heads inside, and I catch the door to follow. Noah looks at me as if for just what he's allowed to say, but I don't have an answer for him. There are no right words to say to my mother, at least none that I've found.

My mother's apartment is worse than it was the last time I was here two years ago. The floors look like they haven't been moped since, and they're caked with dirt. They're darker than the yellow-stained walls from my mother's smoking. There is less furniture, as only a dining room set, a folded-out aluminum futon and a dresser are to be seen around. Dust covers everything, and I wonder if it's enough to suffocate the bed bugs. I come to a stop next to the futon and soon see that that's not the case, as several skitter across the sheet placed over it. One can hope.

"You've gained so much weight," my mother says as she sits down at one of the dining room chairs. She looks older, as her once plump physique has completely sagged into wrinkles and dark spots. I wish she would put some weight back on.

"Same weight that I've been the last ten years," I reply with a smile, trying not to trigger her angry mood.

"So you're pregnant," my mother continues. "I can't see why else you would be marrying, and such a respectable-looking gentleman at that. Deathly skinny as he is. How did you both meet?"

"At the grocery store," Noah says, responding as if it's a question on a game show.

"I see," my mom says and lights a cigarette. I can feel Noah's inner-purity needs screaming. "So what do you work as, Noah?" my mother asks.

"I'm a fashion designer," Noah replies simply.

"So you would have had to have met my daughter at a grocery store," my mother taunts. I don't think she has ever heard how harsh she sounds. "When is the wedding?"

"Likely this summer or late fall," Noah answers again. I have to applaud him for being so cocky to think that he can handle my mom. I smell the coals beginning to heat up under our feet. Soon she will set us on fire and have us running from the apartment in flames. "We would both be honored to have your blessing."

"No," my mom replies, and I can hear the bitterness that has crept already into her voice. "Because this can't work. My daughter can't even take care of herself, let alone a husband— or heaven forbid, a family. She can't keep a job, let alone make herself look presentable for one. I don't know what you see in her."

Noah opens his mouth to speak, but I let out a long sigh, and he takes the hint to shut up.

"Well, Mom, I'm happy to see that you're doing okay. Did you need us to grab you anything with the car?"

"No, I'm fine. Best of luck with your wedding and pregnancy. Just don't bother sending me an invitation for anything," my mother says bitterly.

The whole wedding is a lie, but her words still manage to hurt. I think this is a new record time for unleashing her bitter self too. I thank God that I know now for certain to never, ever bring Caleb here. I lead the way out of the apartment.

"It was nice meeting you, Mrs. Derio," Noah says, trying to keep his cool.

"Same," my mother replies before loudly shutting the door.

Noah is behind me, and we're heading downstairs in the elevator as if we are fleeing a building on fire. "I fail to see the whole point behind that. Was your mother always like that?"

"No," I answer.

"What happened?" he asks curiously as we head towards where he parked the car.

"I stopped being worth a government cheque," I truthfully reply. At least it's a part of the bigger truth.

Noah hesitates to open the car door as he searches for the keys in his pockets. "Hence why you don't flatter easily with money...?"

"Bingo," I reply. I'm about to pull the keys from my back pocket that I had swiped from him in the elevator when I notice a hooded figure. I can't warn him in time when the man suddenly charges at Noah's back and puts a gun to his head.

"Move, and I'll shoot him," the attacker threatens.

Noah only half-glances back and has his hands up in the air.

"Go ahead; you'll be doing me a favor, cause I fucking hate him. But if you want the car, you're going to have to go through me," I say, while lifting the keys I robbed from Noah's pocket for the robber to see.

The car thief smacks Noah hard enough across the side of the head to floor him and goes for me. The moment he's close enough, I grab his gun with both hands, sending a shot off. I push back his fingers till they break the moment the gun falls to the floor. He yells in pain, and I let go of him before I punch him in the throat. I watch him gasp desperately as he falls to his knees on the sidewalk. He's not the first guy I've had to floor in a hurry.

When the red in my vision fades, I run to Noah and pull him back to his feet. I load him into the passenger side of the car after unlocking it, and then I get into the driver's seat. I start up the car, and we're gone.

ELEVEN

Now

Noah moans and then looks at the blood on his hand that is coming from the side of his head. "What the hell just happened?"

"Sorry about that. I didn't know that my old neighborhood had upgraded to carjacking." Inside, I'm worried sick about him. Fortunately, it's just a mild wound he's suffered.

"Unreal," Noah grumbles. "You're crazy. What did you think you were doing attacking him like that? You have some kind of death wish?"

"What? Would you rather I left you bleeding there and run away screaming? Besides, dying isn't hard. Living is," I reply. Noah lets out a long sigh, and I brace myself for what can only be an incoming lecture.

"So, you fight wolves, armed thieves, pickpocket and eat everything for a living. That would explain why I couldn't dig up a whole lot of past on you— you're a superhero. How did you get my keys from my pocket, anyways?"

I shake my head and pull the car over to the side of the road. I don't accept his compliment. Being called a 'superhero' just sounds so weird coming from a guy who could kill someone with one criticism. "You were too distracted with the smell in the elevator." I leave out the part where I was going to use the keys to blackmail him possibly. Only if he had screwed up my already twisted idea of visiting my mother, that is.

"Why did you stop the car?" Noah asks.

"Because I never drove before." I look back and then use the rear-view mirror to make sure I didn't make a roadkill of anything. "It's easier than you make it look."

"You have to be kidding me..." Noah says and flinches in pain as he pulls out his cell phone. He seems to realize that he's in no condition to drive, either. "Caleb is not going to believe any of this."

I wait quietly as Noah calls his brother for help. I swear I can hear Caleb laugh on the other end of the line; as if he had never heard Noah ask for help before. It's very likely.

"He's on his way to drive us far away from here," Noah says and closes his phone. "So...it turns out that I'm too thin and you're pregnant for ten years. Was all of that to fulfill some inner need of yours to be punished and nearly get me killed for real?"

"I had to do that because my mother is usually right."

"You're pregnant?" Noah asks, terrified.

"No, you idiot," I reply and hit his arm. "Not unless I've been pregnant since I was fourteen. But you are too thin.'

"Oh just great. Well then, my equally hypercritical hero, since I can't kiss you, how might I ever repay you for saving my life today?" he taunts.

"With a Big Mac. Actually, make that two Big Macs."

Noah looks at me dumbfounded for a few moments, before coming back around. "Okay then. Junk food it is."

"And you're eating one of them," I add.

"At this rate, it's not like I will get the chance to die from cancer by being around you, so what the hell." Noah closes his eyes as he rests his head against the window. He looks defeated for seemingly the first time in his whole life. "Where did you learn how to do that, anyways?"

"My last foster home."

"They had guns in your foster home?" Noah asks in disbelief.

"No, just my foster-father had one. One of the kids got his paws on it and used to have fun pointing it at me to get what he wanted. Then one day I had enough. I grabbed it out of his hand and pointed it at his head."

Noah was staring at me now, seemingly looking for my lying face.

"Sorry, my true stories all suck," I add. It's the truth.

"What happened then?"

"After what?" I ask.

"When you pointed the gun at his head?"

"They sent me back to my mother's. I could only guess that I had become a level of crazy that they didn't want anymore."

"This was after you got attacked by the wolves?" Noah asks.

His voice has changed to that of deep concern now, and I don't know whether I should trust it or not. So I don't answer.

"Were you born cursed or do you have any happy memories?" he asks, determined to not let me slip out of this conversation.

"I have lots of happy memories. My life wasn't always complete shit," I retort.

"Yet you grew up in that place," Noah says, referring to

my mother's building.

"That place had the best street hockey on the block for your information."

"Let me guess, before they turned it into a real shooting range?" Noah laughs briefly. I think some of my insanity has brushed off on him.

"Whatever," I reply, as he doesn't look likely to fall onto the same page as me at any point in this life.

"If what you say is true, then tell me one happy memory from your childhood," Noah says.

"Swimming. Serious building-wide games of hide and seek. Oh, and my favorite; Chinese restaurant takeovers."

"You mean take-out," Noah tries to correct.

"No, I mean takeovers. Where you and twenty of your friends all pile into some poor Chinese restaurant with the intent to eat everything."

Noah looks out the window as if to visualize such. "Can I ask you a personal question?"

"We're suddenly asking?" I reply.

"After everything you've been through with men, do you even like them anymore?"

The question is unexpected, and I don't have an answer for him. I like one man. The rest in the world could all die for all I cared. Except for maybe Noah. He's proving to be okay.

"Huh," Noah replies, taking my silence as a no. "I've always wondered if there was something that happened in Caleb's past that he never told me. After hearing some of the reasons that make you so complicated, I'm even more worried that I'm missing something important. Has he ever told you anything?"

I remember the long conversations me and Caleb used to have as kids. There wasn't much that we didn't tell each other. Things that we swore to keep a secret, forever.

"Aubree?"

"Uh...you should just ask him," I reply.

Noah rests his elbow on the window and his chin on his hand, looking frustrated at the fact that I won't talk. "I have— dozens of times. He always runs away from my prying without a word. Was his past worse than yours?"

I think about how to word it without betraying Caleb. "Once upon a time I had a happy childhood. Then in the blink of an eye, everything just got turned upside down."

"And my brother?" Noah asks.

"Caleb's life started off as upside down." It's the sad truth. All my sufferings don't even come close to what he's been through.

Noah is studying my face now, and it looks as if he's trying to imagine such a life. The world of the rich seems even more alien to me now. I jump in fright when a knock hits my window. It's Caleb. I open the door and climb between the seats to the emotional safety of the back.

Caleb gets into the car and stares at Noah. "To think all this time I was worried what you were doing to her. Aubree, why's he bleeding?"

"I don't think it's going to be easy to train your brother to fit into the hood," I say, trying to make light of what really happened. "Carjackers are definitely his weak point."

"Carjackers...?" Caleb says as he starts up the car, giving a careful look through his rear-view mirror. "Are we headed home, to the police or the hospital?"

"McDonald's," Noah replies and Caleb hits the breaks before we can pull into the street.

"Did he just say ....McDonald's? Aubree, just how hard did you hit him?" Caleb asks in disbelief.

I laugh as I imagine myself trying to smack Noah upside the head. He's just too tall to so much as think of trying it. "Oh come on. If I could reach that high, the sugar bowl in the top-most cabinet would have been eaten by now." My mind is locked on one word now that I don't want to give up; home. It seems like a distant dream come true. It's only then that I feel something wet and warm between my legs. First I fear the worst as I calculate just when my rag is due. It's weeks too soon. "Um, Caleb?"

"What's up?" he asks, looking in the rearview mirror as he drives.

"Can we pull over to where there's a restroom?"

"Uh, sure."

Noah senses something amiss with my voice and looks back at me. "You okay?"

"I don't know," I say, as I'm feeling extremely terrified and don't know exactly why yet. Nothing in me feels right anymore.

Caleb looks at Noah before pulling the car over to the side of the road.

Noah gets out and opens the back door, and climbs partially into the back to try and figure out what has me so scared. He sees the blood when Caleb puts on the light and is trying to say something, but I can't hear him anymore as his hands pull me out of the car.

TWELVE

Now

Dreams should always remain just out of reach. If you do catch them and they shatter in your hands, then you will have lost what you once reached for to pull yourself out of despair. I used to have a head full of dreams, enough to keep me dreaming at night and daydreaming throughout most of the day. Dreams of being a novelist. Dreams of being happy. Dreams of falling in love. Then in a single day, all my dreams were replaced with a single, desperate wish; the dream of returning home. Little did I know just how hard it would always be for me.

I can feel someone's hand stroking my hair, and it feels nice. It takes a while for me to open my eyes and come around before I quickly remember bleeding in the car. I try to sit up, but a firm hand keeps me pinned down.

"Easy there, Aubree. You can't go running out of here just yet."

I look at Caleb's shaken expression and try to register where I am. "You brought me to the hospital?"

"Where would we bring you?" Caleb asks, trying to keep me calm.

"This is like...so embarrassing... You don't bring a woman to the hospital when she gets her rag. What is wrong with you guys?" I'm embarrassed and confused all at the same time.

Caleb's face turns bright red, but only for a few moments. "Aubree, you were shot in the leg and lost a lot of blood."

I look at Caleb like it's the craziest thing he's ever said. "That's crazy. I would have felt it if I was shot."

"Well, you didn't," Noah says as he comes into my hospital room. There's some dried blood on his shirt and pants. I blink, and the pain finally hits, as if someone had to remind me how to feel it again.

Caleb looks at the IV bag next to my bed and then at Noah. "They have any pain medication in her?"

"They better," Noah says as he leaves the room to go find a doctor.

"I'm officially the biggest pain in the ass in the Universe now," I sulk out loud.

"You saved Noah's life — " Caleb starts.

"I brought him to that horrible place to begin with!" I'm crying now, and it only amplifies the pain that is spreading from my leg to the rest of my body.

"You did nothing wrong by wanting to go and see your mother," Caleb insists.

"Only I didn't visit her for any good reasons. All she does is make me furious and feel ashamed of myself. It's as if I wanted to see her so that I can get high on those hateful feelings in hopes of blocking out everything else. To think it would hit me hard enough this time to keep me from feeling a bullet."

Caleb is wiping the tears out of my eyes, and I fear they might burn him. I can feel his tight grip on my hand. He's rubbing his thumb over the top of it.

A nurse comes in and looks at my IV bag, before sticking a needle in it with some medication. "Let me know if she needs some more in a few hours," the nurse says to Caleb, then leaves.

I let my anger build in me again, and it erases the pain that I'm feeling faster than any pain medication. A part of me wishes that I had never left my apartment the day that started all of this madness. It's bad enough that my life is cursed, but now I've dragged two other people down with me. Then I only have to look at Caleb, and the other half of me screams at the thought of being separated from him again.

"How are you feeling now? Is the medication working?" Caleb asks.

"I'm fine. I just wish I didn't have to put you through all of this." I hear an argument going on outside, and I look as a doctor comes into the room followed by Noah.

"Hello, Miss Derio. How are we feeling?" the doctor asks.

"Miserable," I answer truthfully.

The doctor smiles and takes my clipboard off of the bed. "Just to clarify, which one of these gentlemen is your fiancée?"

Noah is scratching his chin now as Caleb doesn't sense anything amiss. Yet.

"That one is my fiancée, this one is my foster brother," I finish, looking at Caleb.

Caleb frowns at me, and I pinch his hand that he's still holding to keep quiet.

"Any other family?" the doctor asks.

"No," I reply without a second thought. The last thing I need here is my mother laughing at me. How pathetic I am to have been shot on the doorstep of my former building.

"When can I take her home?" Noah asks promptly.

"We've removed the bullet and stopped the bleeding, but I want to keep an eye on her for the next few days. After that, whenever she feels ready."

"What about today?" I ask.

"I wouldn't advise that," the doctor says, and Noah taps his arm, pulling him from the room to talk alone.

The whole scene has me worried, and I wiggle my toes just to make sure I still can. "Caleb, what's going on?"

"Noah is likely making arrangements to get you out of here, today. He doesn't like hospitals."

I look towards the door, wondering what could possibly make Noah scared of a hospital.

"It wasn't long after I was adopted that his grandfather died in this very hospital. He didn't take to it well," Caleb says in answer to the question in my head. "His grandfather had a 'do-not-resuscitate order' on him, and Noah was with him when his heart gave out. Noah wouldn't understand for a long time why no one in the hospital would try to bring his grandfather who was dying before him back to life. From how he's acting now, I can only guess that he still hasn't accepted what happened. It was a horrible day. I can still hear him screaming for someone to help."

"That's horrible," I say, as it hurts to think of Noah in such a state. He's not my favorite person in the world, but neither is he the worst on my list. Especially after how he saved me.

"Your skin is always so cold," Caleb says as he tries to distract me from the topic and rubs my hand in an attempt to warm it up. "They give you all these open garments, and all you need is a pair of mitts and socks for crying out." Caleb is looking in the drawers now in my nightstand as Noah returns.

Noah goes over to my IV and gently pulls the needle from my arm. "Caleb, grab a wheelchair from downstairs. I'll get her dressed."

Caleb leaves to do just that. I look at Noah then as he pulls the blanket off of me as if it were the wrong color tablecloth on a table. I look down at myself to where my gown barely covers my lower parts that lack a pair of underwear. I don't get the chance to defend myself when he pulls the strings on my gown, and I'm covering my chest with my arms. "Hey!"

"Relax," Noah says and picks up my bloody and tattered dress from the nightstand.

One look at it has me feeling even colder. It's irreparably ruined, and I don't want to start guessing what it cost him as he slips it over my head. He's looking around the room again, and I can only guess that it's likely for my panties. I'm completely red now and shaking not only from the cold but from total humiliation. I never took well to anyone touching me, let alone stripping me naked.

When he can't find them, he takes the blanket that had been covering me and wraps me up like a giant burrito. Then he carefully picks me up as if I weigh nothing to him just as Caleb returns with the wheelchair. He sets me down in it, and I can't do much as the blanket is as constrictive as a straight jacket. Despite that, I feel safe again with Caleb guiding the wheelchair. Some pain escapes my leg, but I will it to go away, as I don't want to be stuck here.

I don't protest when Caleb lifts me from the wheelchair and into the front seat of the car once downstairs. I blink as the combined manpower of these two is impressive. It's nice to be taken care of, even though all I have scripted for it all is a meek thank you. Noah looks over my way briefly as he drives away from the hospital parking lot. I continue to sit as a submissive burrito, and I swear that I see him momentarily smile. "I can see you mocking me with your eyes."

"I didn't say anything," Noah says in his defense. "But since you reminded me, thanks for the save."

"Likewise," I mumble back and fall into a comfortable sleep as the pain medication kicks in and puts me out cold.

THIRTEEN

Then

I find myself in a reoccurring nightmare, only today it feels more real. I'm standing in the barn at my second last foster home, staring at a large, empty box. Sapphire isn't here. At first, I was happy to see that she wasn't. I thought that someone must have adopted her while I was asleep. Only, I would find out later that day that my favorite puppy hadn't been adopted but put to sleep. My last connection to anything of worth in my life back then was severed. Maybe I was one of the wolves all along. Maybe they were only sent to punish me for failing one similar to their kind. Maybe they just wanted to bite and curse me for the rest of my life. A snap of teeth wakes me back to the present world.

I'm not wrapped up like a burrito anymore. Instead, I'm sprawled out across Caleb's bed like I own it. I sit up and find that Noah is asleep in his bed a few feet away. I pull my legs over the bed, but I can't get enough courage or strength to attempt standing up. I wonder if this was how Sapphire felt before they carried her away to be executed. Unable to escape anywhere.

"Lie back down before I tie you down," Noah mumbles from his bed, spooking me. He has one green eye open now, watching me.

I look around for Caleb, before remembering that he has a more demanding day job as a mechanic and likely left for it already.

"I'm warning you crazy woman— you try and get up from that bed and starvation will be the least of your worries."

His threat works, and I'm lying back down, covers high over me. Hunger compels me to obey.

Noah moans and rolls out of bed. I only manage half a glance at him before looking away on realizing that he's wearing nothing but boxers.

"Oh don't you start with me," Noah says as he takes notice of my partial glance and walks over to me.

My safety blanket is up in the air and on the floor in the blink of an eye, and I realize that I've been redressed into an over-sized shirt. His hands go for the giant bandage on my leg next, and I have to remind myself how much I hate him to keep from blushing uncontrollably.

Either he doesn't seem to get that he is the opposite sex, or he just doesn't care if it phases me. Gay or not, he could learn to mind his personal space and ask when invading someone else's.

He unwraps my bloodied bandage on my leg. His expression makes it clear that anymore protests out of me won't be tolerated. He wraps a new bandage around and checks that it's not too tight, before throwing my blanket back at me. Noah leaves the room for a moment, then comes back carrying something. It's a McGriddle. I take it from him and rub the wrapping a few times. Then I smell it just to make sure it's real.

"They said they didn't have Big Macs until lunchtime. So that will have to do," Noah states.

"Hey hold on — where's yours?" I ask and look at him.

Noah grumbles at the fact that I remembered the details of our deal, and he leaves and comes back with his own McGriddle. He sits down on the bed with it in hand, waiting for me to eat first. He's acting as if he doesn't know how to tackle his breakfast sandwich without guidance.

I eat slowly, fearing that it could all be a trap. He starts to eat his sandwich in turn and doesn't look to be overly repulsed by it. "Hey Noah, can I ask you a personal question?"

"We're suddenly asking?" he replies, using my words

from earlier against me.

"Why are you such a health nut?"

Noah shrugs. "Comes with the job."

"What about when this is over, and you have your money?"

"Well, it's never going to be over, at least not entirely. Caleb doesn't have the slightest intention of giving you up. So until you guys get your own white picket fence, you get to put up with me. By the way, I'm going to be at a show all weekend. Are you going to be alright alone here with him?"

"Of course. Why wouldn't I be?" I reply.

"Why? Because it doesn't take a genius to see that he's going to jump your bones at the first chance he gets. I don't think that leg of yours is going to slow him down at all. If anything, he'll be less worried of being assaulted should you reject him. You being a cripple now and all."

My face is on fire, and I find myself looking at my half-eaten McGriddle, fearing that I may have burned it.

"Well?" Noah persists.

"Well, what?" I reply.

"You do understand what I'm— ?"

"Yes, I'm not an idiot." It's maddening when he talks to me like I'm some dysfunctional teenager who has no idea how hormones work.

"Because I can take you to the show with me if you want. You are, for the moment being anyways, my fiancée."

I shake my head. "Nope. I'm staying here. Besides, it'll be a good chance to catch up on everything that's happened since me and Caleb have been apart."

"Alright," Noah says, finishing his sandwich and crumpling up the paper in his hand. "Well since we're on the topic, what is it that turns you on anyways?"

My face goes red again, and I'm borderline pissed off now from being embarrassed to death. "Flowers?"

"Not a chance in Hell. You would incinerate them with your eyes. From my limited knowledge of women, I know that they all have something that is particularly unique to them. It's sometimes an art, or just something sexy, and supposedly some are even turned on by intelligent counterparts. But for the life of me, I can't figure out what floats your boat. Aside from your bloodthirsty superhero complex," Noah says.

"Let me guess, whatever I say will be passed on to Caleb at the soonest possible time?"

"You're right. I'm asking something of you for free when I fully intend to use your answer as leverage against my brother. Let's see..." Noah says as he vanishes from the room again and comes back with an old, brown leather journal.

"That's not yours," I say, instantly recognizing Caleb's journal. I'm surprised that he still has it so many years later.

"I won't tell if you don't. Have you ever read it?" Noah asks, flipping quickly through the pages.

I've stumbled over it a dozen times, but I never let myself read it. Caleb told me everything he wanted me to hear and then some. I wasn't going to break our trust by diving into his private writings. "No, and you shouldn't be either."

"Have you ever wanted to?"

"No," I reply without hesitation.

"Why not?"

"Because Caleb trusts me and I'd like to keep it that way. Besides, I know that what gets written on paper doesn't always match what a person's heart is feeling."

"Okay then," Noah says and sulks away. He comes back a few moments later and sits back on his bed. "So just how do I get what I want from you? Shopping? A day at the spa? Slaving myself?"

I start to laugh. "You already have me spoiled on all those counts."

Noah drops his head in defeat.

I know what he's doing, and it's working, cause now I'm feeling sorry for him, and as if I owe him. "August 5th, 2005."

He lifts his head back up and looks towards the other room where he left the journal on the table. Noah returns with it and opens up the book, flipping to the specific date. He reads it over quickly and then looks at me without lifting his head. "You can't be serious?"

I smile and toss my McGriddle wrapper at his head. He takes the hit. "You didn't think I would be easy, did you?" I fluff my blanket then and pull it over myself. I ve earned an extended morning nap.

FOURTEEN

Now

There is a reason why gravity is invisible. Because if we were to see it always weighing us down, day to day, we would lose hope and give up. It doesn't matter that it saves us from being hurled into space and to our deaths; what is important is that it never allows us to be completely free. Most of us are forever earthbound whether we want to be or not. We can never jump high enough to reach the stars or touch the moon. We are bound to be forever below them.

A part of me wants to sleep longer, and the other half of me wants to move around. Playing dead just doesn't seem to have a point anymore. Even if Caleb's sheets smell like cinnamon, just like him. Perfectly edible. I pull myself to a sit and move my legs over the bed. I can see a pair of crutches set out for me nearby, but I still have too much pride to so much as think of using them. I take a deep breath to push back the pain and force myself to stand. I'm a bit wobbly, but manageable, as I pull one leg in front of the other and make my way to the living room.

Noah is sitting on the leather chair, seemingly looking over several photos. "And the zombie apocalypse begins. You hungry again already?"

"Ha, ha. Actually, I just wanted to move around," I say as I sit down on the sofa. "Are these for the show this weekend?" I ask as I look at the photos.

"Yep," Noah replies.

"You look nervous," I say, even though Noah's expression rarely changes.

"Every show does that to me. You can never guess the final word of the critics."

"Well, these all look good so far, and I'm easily your meanest critic," I tease.

"Fair enough," Noah says and picks up the images, before putting them back into his folder and leather bag. "If you're going to wander, you should get dressed as Caleb will be home soon."

I didn't even take notice of my lack of pants till he mentions it. I force back a blush. Apparently, I'm making myself too comfortable for my senses.

"Did you need some help?" Noah asks.

"Oh no— I'll struggle to the last, thank you," I reply, and Noah laughs briefly as I wobble my way back to the bedroom.

"Hey, Aubree?"

I grab the side of the door and look back at him.

"What's up?"

"I didn't stop to thank you yet for doing this little charade. It would seem that we put on such a good show that my parents have already agreed to release the money. Soon, we will be right where we are all supposed to be."

A part of me feels saddened now, and it's coming from the look on his face that he doesn't seem to have a handle on at the moment.

"I think I understand you and what the one thing we have in common now is."

"Oh?" Noah asks curiously.

"You're afraid of being alone and likely hate it as much as I do. You're worried how you will take it should Caleb, and I move out and leave you alone. And I think it all started with your grandfather."

"So Caleb told you about him?" Noah says and looks towards the window.

"Just the sad ending," I reply.

"He was very important to me. Taught me everything I

know about business and life. My parents never really had any time to raise the kids they gave birth to and acquired, sadly."

"I'm sorry."

"I sometimes wonder if they put the do-not-resuscitate order on my grandfather just to spite me out of jealousy. Usually, such a thing is reserved for the frail and sick elderly. My grandfather may have been old, but his heart was as strong as a tank. He shouldn't have had that order to begin with. I still remember the last thing he said to me."

I continue to listen patiently.

"He said that I would find someone who would complete me one day and that when I do, I need to do everything I can to hold onto them. If he were still here, I think the two of you would have gotten along well. You're both natural soldiers."

I smile as Noah is smiling now, and it's a rare sight. It feels like sunlight has just flooded the room out of nowhere. "Is there no one special in your life?"

Noah shrugs and leans back in the chair. "Love is different in my world. It's all about money and power. Being rich is a lot like being king in the old world. You can't just marry whoever you want."

"Your parents were cool with me, though," I add.

"Yeah, that's because they likely dug up your past all the way back to your ancestors and found the same thing I did. Nothing. You're like a blank slate. There isn't anything there for them to object to."

I find that it kinda hurts when someone else lays out the failure of your life before you, but I don't say anything.

"I don't mean that in a hurtful way, sorry," Noah says and then swallows hard.

"It's fine," I reply. I'm more shocked by his apology than his criticism.

"Has your mother ever told you anything about your father? Grandparents maybe?" Noah asks.

"Yes, a bit. My grandparents, if they are still alive, stayed behind in Austria somewhere."

"And your father?"

"My mother says that when it became apparent that I wasn't a boy, he left. That was the end of that."

"I have a hard time believing that," Noah says.

"Well, it's what she said. That's all I know."

"Did you ever want to find him?" Noah asks.

I shrug. 'I think I'm scared that my blank slate version of him is better than what he is in real life."

"Maybe I can find something out about him for you," Noah offers.

"Don't worry about it, Noah. It's like the bottom of my priority list. Heck, it's not even on my list at all."

"Well family, estranged or not, should always be the first on it. Now get dressed before I have to give Caleb a cold shower the moment he enters the door and sees you like that."

I skitter off and close the bedroom door behind me. There is a pair of track pants and a T-shirt on the nearby wooden chair. I'm surprised that either has fallen into Noah's definition of clothes. I head over to them, and my eye catches something white under the dresser. I force myself steady as I lean over to pick it up, and find that it's a white shirt. Only on its collar, is a smudge of red lipstick in a shade I would never wear. I lift it higher and can tell now that it's not Noah's size. I stuff it back under the dresser and get dressed, as a million questions race through my head; the most disturbing one being that I just let myself get duped by my own fairytale scenario, by not one, but two men. I don't feel well on having reached a whole new level of stupid within myself, and I sit down on the edge of Caleb's bed. White picket fence my ass. They could have just told me the truth up front. I stay there until I hear Caleb open the front door on his return home and Noah's voice calls me for dinner shortly after. I get up as the pain in my leg completely disappears from the anger building within me. I stand in front of the long mirror and force the reflection of my soul to cool down. I have to play my cards carefully now as it's obvious I'm surrounded by liars. Ones with power for that matter. Suddenly, Noah's interest in finding my family makes sense. He's looking for a more gentle means of getting rid of me now that he has his money. And Caleb? Caleb was in on the fiancé charade the whole time. I wonder if Noah's attempt to show me Caleb's journal was his way of opening my eyes to the truth.

I laugh at my reflection as I had actually deluded myself into thinking that any of this was real.

"Aubree! Caleb is going to eat your plate if you don't hurry up!" Noah's voice calls from the bar. I step on my anger and leave the bedroom.

"Heya beautiful," Caleb says in greeting. "Good to see you up and walking around. Is the pain any better?"

"It's gone at the moment," I say, and my voice has already started to betray me as Noah pauses in eating. "So, how was work?" I sit down next to Caleb.

"I had to work on a pink Beetle today. I can honestly say there was nothing feminine about that car. We couldn't air out the garage enough," Caleb says and finishes with a laugh.

I smile briefly and look at Noah who has his focus on his food. I take a few bites of the spaghetti, and as always, Noah's cooking is flawless. My stomach screams at me to shut up for the rest of the evening, but it soon proves impossible. "So...now that you guys have the payout, are you going to keep working at the garage? Or you going to get away for a while with your girlfriend?" I ask Caleb.

"I was thinking of getting away for a while. And why didn't you tell me you told her, Noah?" Caleb says as he continues to keep his focus on his food.

Noah's fork falls to the plate rather loudly, and it's enough to get Caleb's complete attention. "How did you figure it out?" Noah's voice is disturbingly low.

"Hermit instincts," I reply, as I continue to eat. Noah is glaring at Caleb now as I have put both of them rather aggressively on the same page. "I'd like to think I'm not completely stupid."

"Why didn't you say something earlier?" Noah asks me. He seems completely toppled.

"Aubree— " Caleb says.

"Just stop," I say, cutting off Caleb. "I'm not pissed off about any of it. Well, maybe the part where you used the whole 'still stuck in puppy love, happily ever after' story on me, but yeah, that's about it. Thank God I don't dupe easily. You could have just told me the truth, Caleb, and I would have followed through with it."

"I didn't lie about my feelings towards you," Caleb says in his defense.

I laugh again and find myself having a hard time finishing my meal, despite being hungry. "Of course not."

Noah has heard enough, and he's on his feet heading to the bedroom. He's intimidating when mad, and I can hear him looking through the room. Then I hear the dresser move.

I'm on my feet now and headed to the door, as I pull free from Caleb's grasp on my hand. It's hard to breathe as I head downstairs and into the open air. Still suffocating, I start walking in no direction in particular. It's cold being early spring, and I curse myself for forgetting my coat. I stop walking at an intersection as lightning flashes across the sky, followed by a boom of thunder. Count on the weather to make my day even worse, as I'm now the centerpiece of its downpour.

A car pulls up in front of me, and I immediately recognize it and the driver.

"Get in the car, Aubree," Noah demands.

"Dream it," I retort and storm off in another direction. Noah gets out of the car and follows me. I want to run, but I can barely keep walking at a speedy pace. He catches up and grabs my arm, which I promptly twist away from. He becomes more determined, and grabs me around my waist next and is carrying me off like I'm his newest handbag.

Kicking and screaming gets me nowhere, as he's just

too strong. Passerby briefly glance at the commotion, but no one seems to care to do anything. "Let me go!"

"No," he replies simply and opens the passenger side of the car, placing me on the seat and closing the door promptly afterward.

FIFTEEN

Now

I may as well have flames coming out of my head as Noah drives us somewhere. He has taken to the highway, which is nowhere near his home anymore. "Where are you taking me?"

"My show is tomorrow, and I won't have you rampaging all over the damn place while I'm working."

"It would be a lot easier if you just drop me off at the shelter because I formally quit this fiancée bullshit."

"What if it wasn't all bullshit?" Noah replies.

I'm having a hard time believing anything out of his mouth at this point.

"Next you're going to tell me that you aren't gay and

have been violating me for the last two months?"

"No, I am gay. I don't feel anything sexually for you or any women for that matter. But that doesn't mean that I don't want to keep you."

"You should have opted for a pet Chihuahua—or a cat."

Noah shakes his head. "I want to keep you, not some animal. Maybe it's selfish, but I don't really care at this point. Somewhere in that head of yours, I know you feel the same way."

"You're out of your mind," I reply.

"Am I? Have you ever stopped to think that you could be worth something to someone past desire?"

I'm laughing now. I spent a good portion of my life living with a man who was an upright-walking pig. I never really cared to think of men in general as anything else. I never encountered one who was anything else. "Yeah, all the time. Give me a break," I say sarcastically. "What's your end game now? Did you not get enough money or something? How much was I worth, anyways?"

"Two million, if you must know."

I'm trying to squeeze all the zeros together in my small brain. They don't fit. "Holy shit. So what compels you to keep me now? Your conscience?"

Noah briefly glances into the rear-view mirror and

then looks at me, looking surprised that I responded to a sentence that included money. "Curiosity."

"Seriously?"

"Yeah," Noah replies. "I never met someone who could show me up at my own game, or so much as keep up with me for that matter. In the very least I find you interesting, only starting with your superhero complex. Granted, your impulsiveness could use some taming."

I drop my head against the side of the window. The pain is coming back from my leg, which can only mean that he's breaking my defensive anger. "Why couldn't you just tell me the truth after you got your money?"

"Because I wasn t ready to lose you, and I knew you would run out the door the moment Caleb's illusionary love for you faded." He digs into his pocket and pulls out a silver figure, then puts it on my lap. He takes brief notice of the blood that has seeped through my bandage and into my rain-soaked gray track pants.

I look at the silver figure and see that it's a knight in full armor, holding a spear. I pick it up and remember when Caleb gave me something familiar, only it was a knight with a sword.

"Look, I see that you want a happy ever after ending to your life, but that's not what you need right now. Right now we need each other. Even if you are a bloody hurricane to keep up with. Literally." He puts his hand on my leg and quickly assesses the damage while maintaining an eye on the road at the same time.

I close my eyes as I give in to defeat. My brain screams at me that I've let myself become a prisoner all over again, while my heart seems remarkably calm about it all. Waging war against the whole damn world is exhausting when one is going on inside yourself. I stay awake as we pull into a motel and Noah orders me to stay put while he checks us in.

He comes back a few minutes later and opens my door. "You okay to walk?"

The pain is back in its entirety now, and I'm not sure. I pull my legs out of the car and try to muster the strength to stand up, but it's not happening. I wonder if depression can hit this damn fast to weigh me down.

Noah doesn't give me much time to figure it out as he scoops me up and carries me to our room. It's utterly romantic — if I didn't hate him almost as much as I hate myself. He opens the door and picks me back up, carrying me to the side of the bed where he sets me to a sit. Locking the door behind us, he pulls off his jacket and tosses it to a chair. "You've gone quiet on me. Other than bleeding out, you alright?"

I don't answer as he strips me from my track pants and reveals my bloody bandage. He takes it off and then tosses it in the trash.

"The doctor says you can't have a bath with that wound. You okay with a shower?" he asks.

I don't answer.

"Well," Noah says as he looks to weigh his options, "I won't have you falling asleep soaked and bleeding." He heads over to the bathroom and starts up the shower.

Running is impossible as is fighting as he threatens to strip and carry me before I force myself to my feet and my own shower. He watches me like prey as if I might climb out the tiny bathroom window that is half the size of my ass in some escape attempt. I get my T-shirt off and have just set my head under the running water when he finally disappears.

He isn't gone for more than a few minutes, and when I look back at the bathroom door, he's back and has his clothes off. I burn up. I ready myself to start a screaming fit at him, but I'm terrified out of my mind, and I don't know if he intends to rape me.

He steals the shower head and pulls the hose down, and blasts my face with it. "You should know by now that I'm not going to hurt you."

I try to relax, and as my eyes try to find somewhere to safely look, I take note that he doesn't seem to be the slightest bit aroused by my naked presence. I'm the weird now one as I'm the only one freaking out. It's fading, though, as he gently washes my hair, taking care not to touch me with anything other than his hands. He does take a particular interest in my scars from my encounter with the wolves as his fingers trace a few on my back. A quick soap down after, and he grabs a towel and lets me out of the shower before dropping it on my head.

I don't look back as I wobble my way to the bed while drying off and Noah continues his shower. I'm surprised to find a duffle bag on the bed. I figure that he got it before joining me in the shower. I take my chances peeking into it. It looks like a few sets of clothes for both of us and a roll of bandaging. I pick that up and sit down on the side of the bed. I'm only halfway done with it when Noah comes out of the shower with a towel around his waist and finishes the wrapping for me. He leaves a long tail on the bandage for some reason.

"Your leash so you don't disappear in the night on me," he explains.

I sigh. It's not like I can run or drive anywhere. He helps me get dressed in another oversized shirt, before slipping into a pair of dry boxers for himself. Then he tucks me in, but not before wrapping the tail of my bandage a few times around his hand and settling down beside me. I find myself staring back at him for a long while, and he seems content to do the same. "I won't run away. It's not like I can."

"Can't be too sure with you. Plenty of conventional superheroes can fly, after all. Now get some sleep." He rolls onto his back and pulls the blanket higher over him, and checks my leash with a gentle tug.

I curl up and let myself fall asleep. Despite the nightmare run I've been on, I don't dream.

SIXTEEN

Now

I know that I've been deprived for too long from positive human contact when I wake up with Noah's arm around me. Instead of having a panic attack, I stay quiet and absorb some of his heat for a while. I feel like I'm the perverted one, knowing full well that he doesn't have any interest in me, and yet here I am taking full advantage of his touch. He wakes up and rolls over, seemingly unaware of the fact that he was just cuddling me, or he's just good at pretending that he wasn't. "Morning," I say as he lets out a loud yawn.

"Mornin'," he says and sits up. "You sleep okay?"

"Peachy," I reply, trying to sound bitter. But it's mostly my hunger talking. He's turning my brain and sense of logic into a complete mush. It's getting harder and harder to stay mad at him.

Noah gets up and pulls me out an outfit from the duffle, before finding his own. We get dressed without talking and are headed outside for the car after he is dressed to kill in a black suit and white shirt. I get a flashback of when he spoke to me outside the homeless shelter, and I find myself wondering if he really did go back home afterward. He has already proved himself to be a stalker.

"What did you want for breakfast?" he asks.

I glance out the window as we're near the city's core and there are a few options. "I don't know."

"Well you better make up your mind, or you're eating my breakfast," he says as he digs through the duffle bag stuffed between the seats at a stoplight. He pulls out a tray of whole grain toast, carrots, celery and what looks like some kind of homemade granola bar.

I dart my gaze back out the window in terror of missing my breakfast for the day, just as he taunts my nose with the granola bar.

I get fed up, and I snatch it from him. He's all eyes on me at another stoplight as I take a bite. It's not half bad. Then again, I'm an idiot to think that it's bad, as he's never cooked or baked the sorts.

He's laughing now as if he just crossed off something from his mental bucket list.

"Spare me," I say.

"I'll take you out to dinner later and replace your missing calories, I promise. We're just in a hurry now, and this traffic isn't co-operating."

I pack down the rest of the granola bar. "Did I need to know anything important for this? I've never been to a fashion show before."

"Well, there's going to be a lot of people there, and from Caleb's diary, I can only guess that you likely still hate crowds. So I thought that I stuff you in the back to get powdered and pretty by one of my guys until it starts. Then you can come out and sit near the middle if you want. My parents are likely going to be in the front row so you can hide just behind them."

"Alright," I say and watch as he pulls into an underground garage. A valet takes the keys from Noah as we exit the car and I follow closely behind him as we enter the hotel. It's all lights a glamor, and it doesn't take long for me to feel out of place. People start to recognize Noah almost immediately, and I get my shit together as the fiancé he introduces me as. We head to the back where the event looks to be staged in one of the halls, and it's already packed with women getting ready, and people running about.

Noah takes my hand as I begin to feel overwhelmed and sits me down in one of the makeup chairs. "Gregory, I need you over here."

I look as a shorter, bald man comes over my way and greets Noah in an overwhelmingly friendly fashion with a kiss on the cheek.

"This is my fiancé, Aubree," Noah says. "Aubree, this is Gregory, my best makeup artist. He's going to get you pretty and show you around. Nothing red, no bold prints, and whatever you do— don't let her out of your sight. I gotta whip some slackers around here."

"Of course, Boss," Gregory says.

"You be good," Noah instructs me and then hastily walks off.

"Ah, so I get the fiancé all to myself. It's an honor," Gregory says as he starts to wipe down my bare face. "You must tell me all your secrets."

"Heh," I reply, wondering if Gregory was ever in a relationship with Noah. I don't want to step on the wrong toes. "Can't say what he sees in me."

"Oh, nonsense. You have such lovely hair and skin. And your blue eyes," Gregory says as he lifts my face to align with his, "so pretty."

I raise an eyebrow, hoping that he doesn't strip me bare and see just how not-nice my skin is. I want to tell him that I'm immune to most flattery, but instead, I give an appreciative smile. I look over at the models getting ready, and I can't help but envy them. They're a fraction of my size, and any one of them could make Caleb look twice at them. I knew that I was way out of my league at the start, but by being here, I feel as if that fact has been superimposed forever with my less-happier memories.

"Did you want the pink one or blue?" Gregory asks as he holds up two dresses before me.

I take a moment to return my attention to him and look at the blue dress. "That one, please."

"It will bring out your eyes nicely," he says and hands me the dress, before ushering me over to a private stall to change.

I close the curtain behind me and slip out of my jeans and sweater, and into the dress. It has the effect of making me feel better, as I look in the mirror to where my makeup and hair are already set to perfect. I come out of the change room and set my old clothes down on my chair. Gregory has vanished on me.

I look about as everyone is busy and stressing, and decide to show myself around as I sneak out of the commotion and find myself in an emptier and airier hallway. I circle and come to the front of the hotel, before making my way back inside. I find a cozy seat in the middle, and amongst the slighter lower-classed in society. I catch a glimpse of Noah off to the side, and as if sensing me, he turns around. He sees me, and satisfied that I haven't run off anywhere, he returns to work.

"Oh no no, you have a seat reserved for you at the

front."

Gregory catches my hand by surprise and is pulling me from my seat and to the front. To make matters worse, he sits me right next to Mrs. and Mr. McCowan, Noah's parents. I feel like running for the door.

"Oh, Aubree, it's so good to see you again," Mrs. McCowan says as she turns to me. "How are you?"

"I'm great," I reply. "How have you been?"

"Oh, busy as usual. It seems the stock market won't let me sleep just yet."

Mrs. McCowan continues to chatter, and I continue to listen. After a while, I feel like I'm being stared at, and I turn my gaze to the other side of the catwalk. There's a man with dark, short curls staring at me, and he doesn't look to be the slightest bit happy. I search my memory for if I ever saw him before, but I have none.

He gets up and walks around, before coming towards my seat. After dropping a large envelope into my hands, he storms out of the hotel.

I look at the envelope, and in sensing nothing good, I excuse myself from Noah's parents and head back to the hallway that was relatively quiet. I look the envelope over, before opening it. There are several pictures inside, and it doesn't take much before I see exactly what they are pictures of. Noah clearly had a relationship with this creepy guy, and he made a thing of photographing much of their bedroom life. I can only guess that he gave me this envelope to break off an engagement that only I, Noah, and Caleb know isn't real. I'm flaming mad now as I tear the envelope and pictures into unrecognizable pieces. I toss them into the garbage, before heading to the front of the hotel.

I find the creep and grab him, giving him little choice but to follow me as I drag him away to the alleyway next to the hotel. Once alone, I kick him in the balls, before punching him across the face with all my rage. He falls to the ground, and I'm on top of him now with my fist ready to deck him another one. He tries to call for help, but I have my other hand over his mouth, and it silences him. "You piece of shit need to take your little jealous streak somewhere else before I make you completely unrecognizable. You seem to be confused to just who I am." I hold him still as he tries again to struggle. "Now do yourself a favor and fuck off to another country." I climb off of him, and he scrambles in pain to his feet, before making his way to where his fancy car is waiting for him. I wait for him to drive away before breathing again. Then I try and collect myself for a few minutes. My werewolf mode is always hard to shake off.

"Aubree! What are you doing out here!?" Gregory is frantic. "How did you get dirty? You had me worried sick! The show is about to start!" He's cleaning the dirt off of my dress with his hand now before he pulls me back into the hotel.

I barely acknowledge anyone as he sits me back down, and Mrs. McCowan fails to regain my attention. My humanity returns near the end of the fashion show, and my rage finally boils down to a simmer. It's a good show, but I already know this as Noah has shown me most of the pictures for it.

I don't move on my own when it's over with an overwhelming applause. Instead, I sit and wait patiently for Noah to be done and hopefully come and get me. I have no idea whether I should tell him what happened, or shut up. This is a happy day for him, and I don't want to ruin it.

"Aubree," Noah says and is standing in front of my chair. "You're looking dazed and confused. You alright?" He takes my hand and pulls me to my feet. "Did you like the show?"

"That was amazing," I say with a smile. "I got positive vibes from everyone else too." Everyone but one person.

He wraps up his commands with his team with a quick run through backstage before leaving the hotel with me.

SEVENTEEN

Now

I'm unusually quiet on the car ride home, and Noah can sense something is up. But I'm having a hard time making conversation with the potential consequences of what I did still simmering in my head.

"Alright, what did you do?" he asks.

"Nothing," I reply. And I'm still bad at lying.

"Aubree..."

"I...uh..." I clear my throat. I un-crumple a small piece of a photograph that I saved, mainly of the man's face who I attacked at the show. "Do you know him?"

Noah frowns for a moment as he glances my way to look at the torn picture while keeping his eyes on the road. "Where did you get that?"

"I saw him at the show. He was looking at me all angry-like."

"Did he give you this?" Noah asks in concern.

I break under the increasing pressure. "He gave me a whole envelope of photos. I think his plan was for me to go all ape-shit on you at the show and ruin it for you, being you fiancé and all."

Noah pulls over to the side of the road, and there are a few minutes of silence between us before he speaks again. "Just what was in these photos?"

"Uh... Nothing that I would pin up, that's all."

Noah nods once and then rests his elbow on the window. It's become a habit for him for when he's hurt. "I wish you didn't see any of that."

"It's fine, Noah. I mean, I didn't look at them closely once it was clear what they were. Either way, it's unlikely that he will be bothering you anymore."

"Oh?" Noah asks and looks at me.

"I might have accidentally beat the crap out of him in the alleyway next to the hotel."

"Seriously? You took on a full-grown man by yourself?"

"That wasn't a man; it was a monster. Hopefully, I

won't get any assault charges, and we're peachy," I say and add on a somewhat reassuring smile. It's not working, as I'm thoroughly terrified that I'll see assault charges at some point down my miserable road.

Noah starts up the car and looks in the rear-view mirror as if fearing the police might be behind us. "Remind me to spot my ex's before you do. You can't keep putting yourself in danger like that."

"Hey, you wouldn't have done anything less if the pictures were of me."

Noah lowers his head as it's the truth. His expression suggests that he would go the extra mile and commit murder.

I'm rather surprised by his reaction. It's been a long time since I felt that another person cared about my well-being.

"I can't even begin to think of the crap I'd be getting now if that envelope had have landed in my parent's hands — or the media's," Noah says.

"You're changing the subject," I interject.

"No, you're trying to make this conversation about something else. Heck, just talking about those pictures has turned your face completely red."

I touch my cheek and find that he's telling the truth. Dammit. I hate Noah for being able to burn me with what should be his own burn.

He laughs briefly and shakes his head. "You're not allowed to fall in love with me. You're only allowed to hate me. I should have made that clearer, sooner."

"Fine. I still hate you. And I seriously fucking hate those blue and green underwear you apparently own. I suggest you start hiding all your scissors." I finally got him by the balls now as his face flushes red, and he's looking completely flustered. "And just to prove how much I hate you, we're going to Taco Bell for dinner."

Noah gulps as he turns the car in the direction of the mall. "Is this going to be worse than that Griddle thing?"

"Oh yeah. Stupid health nut. Your kind will drag you out into the street and burn you at the stake as a traitor by the time I'm through with you."

"Ouch," Noah replies. "Would that make you feel better?"

"Maybe."

"By the way, thanks for the save today. I think I might be indebted to you for the rest of my life at this rate," Noah says.

"You're welcome," I grumble back and rest my head back to catch a nap. People always exhaust me, and I know I sound grumpier than I want to.

Noah pats my head and finishes with a short laugh. My

grumpy mood doesn't deflect him in the least. "My own pet bodyguard. I never thought that an introvert could excel at that kind of occupation. You're full of surprises, crazy woman."

I close my eyes and wonder just how long that part of me can remain a good thing.

EIGHTEEN

Then

Creation's greatest illusion is love. The idea of someone else caring about you. The idea of never being alone. The hope of something more than the monotonousness repetition of everyday life. Without it, we would lack a powerful driving force to go on against all the forces that work tirelessly against us. It's only when you see through this lie that is love, does the brutal truth become so real and unbearable. It was also the only thing I had to grab onto at one point.

Back then it had all happened so fast that it had paralyzed me. I sat unbelieving in the chair at the Children's Aid Society one summer morning, staring out the window where the birds chirped outside in tune to the beautiful day. I didn't hear any of it. I had been beaten, I had run, and now I was here to serve my time for who knew how long. My sentence for being a coward had begun.

I looked at my temporary social worker as she walked over to me. She was a good foot shorter than I was, but she would become one of the most intimidating people I had ever known. Everything about this place screamed wrong. Even as the bruises on my arms began to turn purple, their pain was nothing compared to the fear in me now. I had heard the stories; kids who got shipped off to foster care didn't get out. Ever. Now as the woman began to speak I found that I still couldn't hear anything. All I heard was my racing heartbeat that hadn't caught up to the fact that all of this was happening to me.

After taking my silence as an 'I heard you but am not going to respond,' my worker turns around and leaves me alone in the waiting room again. Alone. That I was for certain. My mother had transformed into a violent stranger, and I was too slow to put the scale of my life against her drinking back into its precarious balance. My friends were far away. My home was back there with them, and no one here gave a damn about me. The Society's only concern was finding someone they could shove me onto. All it had taken was one phone call from my mother. She thought that I had run away from home when I was only running from her. Remembering nothing of her own drunken state, my argument was a lie to her ears. To her I didn't run away because she had turned violent, but because I was being a bad kid.

I remember telling myself over and over that I wasn't a bad kid. Foster care was for bad kids. I had nothing to be scared of and nothing to hide. My mother would get a break from me, and I would go home soon, and everything would be as it was. And if it weren't, I would have learned my lesson and not be stupid enough to cry for help a second time. People may listen, but they never truly heard you. This is what I would come to learn shortly after I was shipped off to my first foster home. I thought that I had it all figured out. Then he happened.

Someone is petting my hair, and it feels nice. I feel wet, and I realize that I'm sweating from the nightmare I had. I sit up and try to see in the absolute darkness of the room. I can feel Noah looking at me.

"You alright? You were having another nightmare," Noah says in a concerned whisper.

My eyes adjust to the darkness and I see that Caleb's bed in the room is empty. He's been missing too much lately, and it worries me. If he keeps it up, I'm likely to become frantic. He may never become my dream boyfriend again, but I'm not ready to sever him out of my life as a friend.

"He's out for the night," Noah explains.

I tug my hair behind my ear as my eyes adjust to the dim lighting in the room.

"What was it about?" Noah asks.

"Huh?" I ask as I lie back down.

"Your nightmare."

"Just the lousy day I was taken from my mother."

Noah rolls over to face me. "Did you need a snack?"

"I'm all right," I say as I pull the blanket over me. He didn't undress me this time, as I'm still wearing my blue dress. On realizing that, I get back up and grab a shirt and track pants from the duffle bag on the floor and head to the washroom to change. I feel as if I ruined enough pretty clothes to risk ruining this dress too. I return and am left with the awkward choice of stealing Caleb's bed or returning to Noah's. It doesn't matter that I know it's all a lie, cause I don't care anymore. I go back to Noah's bed, and he tucks me in. I curl up closer to him, and he doesn't seem to mind. He sets his hand back on my hair, content to continue petting me like I am his pet. To hell with details and consequences of said title; being a pet has its perks. Even though it will be harder to convince myself down the road that none of this was for real.

NINETEEN

Now

I have a bad feeling when Noah pulls me out of the house the next day before I can so much as manage a yawn. Part of me is feeling scared again, as I think that he might be dragging me to the police station to make me take responsibility for my assault the other day. I wasn't going to run this time. Prison didn't look as scary as the option of freezing on the street. "Where are we going?"

"There's something I've been working on for you," Noah replies.

"What?"

"Well," Noah continues, as he briefly glances at me while continuing to drive, "I used a few of my contacts to see if I could track down your dad."

"Please tell me you're kidding..."

"Don't be mad. It's none of my business if you choose to hate him for all eternity, or just kill him on the spot. I have your back regardless of what you want to do. What I'm more interested in is getting you financially independent."

"You can't be serious..." I say. "I'm not a kid anymore. My window for child support is long gone."

"Clearly you have never met my lawyer," Noah replies with a grin on his face.

"This is stupid. It will never work," I say confidently, and cross my arms before me.

"Why?" Noah asks.

"Because it's just stupid."

"You don't have to be scared. I'm going to be right there with you. Heck, I might even end up hitting him first."

"I don't care about collecting money from my deadbeat father. I don't give a shit at all about him."

"Don't you want to know at least why he left you? Because the answer your mother gave you doesn't sound like the truth," Noah says.

I look out the window as we pull up in front of some fancy house. "And of course he would live here... Please, let's just go home. I don't want to do this."

"Oh, you're not going chicken out on me now," Noah says as he gets out of the car and comes around to the passenger's side. "Let's go. You can rage all you want on me afterward if you want."

I get out of the car, but it's not until he's towing me behind him that I start walking. We go through the perfectly groomed front lawn and up the stairs to the fancy double white doors. I don't feel well, and I can only guess that Noah has left me hungry for this so that I stay in attack mode.

Noah rings the bell and keeps a tight grip on my hand.

An older, blond woman opens the door and greets us, and Noah asks for a Mr. Ferin. She disappears for a moment, and a man comes down the stairs. His hair is mostly gray and slicked back, and wrinkles surround his eyes. He's tanned like he just got back from some beach in the Bahamas.

"How might I help you, young lady?" he asks after Noah diverts his attention to me.

I have no fucking clue what to say. I didn't have so much as any time to rehearse. "Do you happen to know a Ms. Derio?"

The man looks unnerved by the question, and I have my answer.

"I'm sorry, but I don't," Mr. Ferin replies.

I can see now where I get my eyes from and my awful lying. Bastard has the same nose as me too. I feel like smacking it off of his face.

Noah pulls out his cell phone and drags down his latest text messages. "You knew her for about four years until she got pregnant and you left a month after Aubree here was born."

"Look, I don't know what you both want, but I don't have any children," Mr. Ferin says defensively and closes the door in our faces.

"And there you have it," I say and start back towards the car.

Noah follows me, but he's on the cell phone talking to someone. I stand on the passenger side of the car, as he seems to be taking his time. Instead of opening the car, he leans against it.

"What are we doing?" I ask. I can't stand being here anymore.

"Just wait for it," Noah says and then nods in the direction of the house.

I look the same way and see my supposed father scrambling down the stairs and walking briskly towards us in his house slippers. Mr. Ferin looks furious.

"I'm not paying any child support. Your threats on the

phone will not intimidate me."

"Even after you so skillfully dodged it when Ms. Derio took you to court? How convenient for you that she couldn't afford to have a DNA test done to confirm that you were the father."

"I'm not this woman's father— !"

"Look, asshat," Noah interrupts, and his voice has become deadly serious, "we can play this game all you want. I have all kinds of time, and my lawyers have been bored as of late. That and I'm willing to put my money down that my lawyers can very quickly run yours into the ground before you can make a phone call. My fiancé wants answers, and you're going to stop being an irresponsible loser, or you're going to be doing a lot of explaining in court. I'm sure your wife would be interested in all of this as well."

I'm stumped as Noah has me officially intimidated, and I'm not even the target. It seems to be working on my father too.

"What do you want?" Mr. Ferin asks.

"You left me after I was born. Why?" I ask. My fear has been replaced with anger, as Noah's courage is contagious.

"Things were complicated at the time. It wasn't working out with your mother."

"But that isn't the only reason you bailed, is it?" Noah says, looking at the window where Mrs. Ferin is looking out. "You were seeing someone else at the time. Someone more profitable."

"Is there anything else?" Mr. Ferin asks, getting increasingly agitated with how Noah is watching the window.

"Just that my lawyers will be in contact with you. Thank you for your time," Noah says, and he heads around to the driver's side of the car.

I feel too sick to so much as look at my supposed father and get into the car.

"Wait," he says and holds my door. "How much is this going to cost me?"

"To what? Make me disappear?" I ask.

"Yes," Mr. Ferin replies.

I look at the house and ponder just how much the asshat is worth. "My mother is living in a complete shithole for the last twenty-five years. Whether it's because of you or not, I don't care. I can't help her as unfortunately I'm the only one she's had to blame for her miserable life, and she won't let me. So set her up with something better, and you will never have to see me again."

"That's all?" Mr. Ferin asks.

"You're nothing and no one to me, so I want nothing." I pull the car door closed and look ahead. I don't want to look at him anymore. I wish my brain would just run away from me before it can explode.

"You sure?" Noah asks. "We can easily get a million out of that prick."

"Taking money from him would acknowledge that he exists. And to me, he doesn't. I'm happier if we can keep it that way," I reply, without looking at Noah.

Noah lets out a sigh and starts up the car for home. "You're the boss."

TWENTY

Now

Noah is feeling personally responsible for my mood as he makes a stop at a bakery downtown. A few minutes later he hops back into the car with a bag. He hands it to me, and I peek inside. "Pecan tarts?"

"You have to eat something. Your hunger strike is worrying me," he says.

I look inside the bag again, but my appetite isn't there. Any faith I had in the male species has just been burned away. I feel sick in thinking that it's possible for me to be even more alone than I started off this life as.

Noah reaches inside the bag and offers to hand feed me. I give in and take a bite.

"Phew," he says and puts the remaining tart back in the

bag. "Well, we still have the rest of the day. We can go anywhere you want."

I glance at him, unable to think of any place I want to be right now.

"Okay, then I have an idea. And you're not allowed to hate it."

I'm worried again as he makes another phone call. His codes and use of another language is confusing, and I can't figure out his next evil plan for me. We don't drive far afterward, and I'm surprised when we pull up at the pool near the beach. "Oh hell no. I can't swim."

"Of course you can swim. You're a several medal and ribbon winner."

"That's not what I mean. What I mean is that I can't wear a bathing suit."

Noah just laughs and gets out of the car. "I packed one for you."

Damn that evil duffle bag. After I'm done cutting his boxers to shreds, I'm burning that bag. I didn't take the swimsuit garment I spotted inside seriously until now. But I don't budge, even when he opens my door.

"Hey, you trust me, don't you?" Noah asks.

"No," I answer flatly.

"Okay, okay, so I've been cruel to you for too long. But

this idea is a winner, I swear," Noah promises.

"I can't wear a bathing suit."

"You stubborn little donkey," Noah says and drags me out of the car by force, then locks the doors. He pulls me behind him, and we head inside. He doesn't stop at the women's change room.

"Noah, are you crazy?" I ask. I fear an uproar if there are any women inside.

He hands me my bathing suit and stands right next to the door to prevent my escape as he changes into a pair of swim shorts.

"You clearly want to die," I say.

"Better hurry up, or you're going to have to take on the women who freak out on seeing me."

"Unreal," I say, and I choose a private stall to slip into my light blue bathing suit. I set my clothes down on the bench and look around, fearing that our luck is burning up with the chances of someone coming in. My eyes are locked on the mirror in the change room as my scars can be seen, at least one covering every part of my body. I don't get to look long, as Noah is dragging me out to the indoor pool. It's surprisingly empty, without so much as a lifeguard on duty.

He picks me up and drops me into the water before I can try and escape him. Then he dives in. I come back to the surface, swearing to drown him. But he's already trying to swim away. I swim after and corner him, and he tries to swim past me, but I got him around the neck now. It's a futile move, as he's just too tall and too strong. He throws me into the water like I'm nothing.

"Damn it," I say as I come back to the surface. "That's cheating!"

"What?" he taunts me. "I thought you were a superhero?"

"I will kill you!" I splash him, hoping to wash some of the bullshit off of his face, but that only gets me tackled again. And again. Finally, I give up and try to swim away in defeat. This one I almost win, as I do manage to hit the deep end's wall with my hand before he's pulling me backward to make it look like he won the race. I grab onto the wall again, eyeing the center rope in the pool with the thought of strangling him with it.

"I'll race you," Noah says between his laughing.

"You're too tall," I reply.

"I'll give you a head start."

"Fine," I reply and push off the wall, and start for the shallow end. I take half a peek back a third of the way across and watch as he pushes off the wall and comes after me like a tsunami. I speed up, and I am almost out of the deep end when he speeds past me. It's then that a cramp takes my leg and forces me to a dead stop in the middle of the water. My momentary panic from the pain and paralyzation sends a rush of water into my lungs, and I'm gasping before I can force myself to calm down and try to tread to stay afloat.

Noah grabs me and pulls me to the side, and holds onto the wall with his other hand as he tries to figure out what's wrong with me. "You alright?" he asks as he holds me tight.

"Stupid leg cramp," I grumble. I feel like a drowned rat that can't even swim right. I'm am officially the most miserable one on the planet right now.

He lets out a breath of relief. He leaves me on the side and pulls himself out of the water, before lifting me up and out. He pulls some of my hair out of my eyes to get a fix on my current level of pain. "Geez woman, you scared the life out of me. You gotta stop doing that."

"I blame your pecan tart." I cough the rest of the water out of me before returning to sulking.

"I blame all the ones I didn't feed you," he teases.

I manage to sit all the way up, but he pulls me into a protective hug which I find strange, but warming. It occurs to me then that the pool is still empty. "How did you scare everyone out of the water, anyways?"

"Heh, I don't know what you're talking about."

"You're positively evil," I say.

"Well that's your fault because I have no idea how else to keep up with you," he says into my ear.

With him so maddening close, I can't find the strength to get to my feet. I may as well be a cripple under his touch. He gets up some minutes later and grabs a towel from the bench, and wraps me up in it before grabbing one for himself.

I won't admit it, but despite the cramp, the swim has me feeling refreshed. In the least, it's doused all the energy I was burning away with my anger. I had forgotten how much I loved the water, and I reluctantly waddle after Noah as it's time to leave. I slip into the private stall again and get changed as he changes outside. The back of my head is worried about the war that will ignite if a woman were to walk in now and see him changing. I get dressed faster.

TWENTY-ONE

Now

"So you and Noah are a thing now?"

Noah is unusually missing and I find myself alone with Caleb that morning. I don't have much of an answer to give him. "We are...friends. I think." I sound so lame.

"Well, I have to admit I'm surprised. I didn't think Noah would ever spin that way."

"Who says he has? Who says I'm even interested?"

Caleb puts down his glass of water to study me for a moment. "Guys suddenly not your thing?"

"Guys stopped being my thing a long time ago." It comes out a lot harsher than I want it to.

"Maybe you just never met the right guy."

"Like who? You?" Our conversation is escalating into a fight, and my emergency breaks are screeching in my head. "Look, Caleb. The joke is over now, okay? You don't have to explain or pretend anything. Nor do you have to feel like you have to change me. I'm not a kid anymore. I know what I want."

"Fair enough," Caleb says, then finishes off his water. "But have you thought about what will happen when one of you want something more? Gays don't turn straight, and you're not lesbian or asexual as far as I can tell."

"Why? Because I blush at the presence of a pretty guy? Well shit, I need to work on that then." I jump down from the bar stool.

"It's not all about you, you know? I don't want to see my brother get hurt."

"I have no intention of hurting either of you. I can hold my sexual impulses just fine. Hell, it's all I've been doing for the last ten years."

Caleb walks over to me and catches my face with his hand. But I don't react. My mind is still locked on Noah, and I see now how it has made me stronger. The ice wall I've built around my heart isn't melting under Caleb's warm touch.

"What happened to you after I left your life?" Caleb asks. His tone is serious.

I don't answer him.

"You can tell me, Aubree. You need to tell me because whatever it is, it's eating you alive. I care about you, and nothing you do is going to be able to change that." He takes his hand away and grabs his jacket before heading out.

I find myself alone in the apartment, and it's a deafening kind of silence. I roam around the place, with no particular direction, before my eyes catch sight of what looks like a phone bill. I pick it off of the shelf and quickly look at the last few numbers and see that it's Noah's. None of the names or numbers ring familiar, except for one. Curiosity keeps me going and I open Caleb's laptop and decide to Google the number. To my surprise, it's the Children's Aid Society. Suspecting that one of the brothers is digging into my past, I Google some more of the numbers until a familiar face shows up on the screen. One that I will never forget.

I find my wallet on the table and run out the door. Everything screams wrong as I feel that Caleb and Noah are about to do something irreversibly stupid. Neither of them should be out at this hour. Once outside, it takes me a few minutes to hail a cab, and I send him to the address that I saw on the computer.

It takes several minutes to get there, and I order him to stop as I see Noah s car outside a house. I pay the cab and leave it. I cross the street, but I hesitate to go any closer to the house. I stand behind the shrubs of another house several lawns away and wait. I don't know what I'm waiting for, but it becomes clear when Noah and Caleb leave the house they're parked in front of in unison. They drive off, and I emerge from the bushes.

I run to the house and around the back. Not seeing anything, I get on my knees and peer through the basement window. Someone is on the floor, curled up in pain. It takes a while to realize who it is through all the blood on his face. I stand up and back away from the house, before starting in the direction of home. I feel cold as it's clear that Noah and Caleb are taking what happened in my past way too far in the future. I spent my whole life running from my past, and now it was all being dug up and kicked my way. I don't know what to do or think anymore, and I just keep walking, hoping that I can burn the horrible feeling inside me before I reach home.

❊ ❊ ❊

It's an hour later, but I'm almost home when I pass a bakery. In need of an excuse to where I was, I go inside. I look around before a simple croissant gets chosen. I pay and leave, and continue home. I finish my croissant and stop to take in my reflection in a piece of metal on a post. I've been crying, and I don't see it until now. I rub the tears off of my face and try to get my shit together. I barely have a moment to before a pair of hands touch my shoulders and startles me.

"Hey," Noah's voice says.

"Noah," I say and pretend to brush the croissant crumbs off of me. "I've been caught. Dammit."

He shakes his head and wipes a crumb off of my face. I hope that he can't see that I've been crying. I smell blood and dare a peek at his knuckles. They're red and bloody. Like he just got out of a fight, because he did. "What happened to your hands?" I ask and grab one.

"It's nothing," he says defensively and pulls his hand away. "Caleb taunted me that I couldn't fix a car for the life of me, and naturally I get my hand stuck trying."

It's an impressive lie, but still a lie.

"And seeing as I can't keep you from running around without a leash, I got you this," Noah says and hands me a small bag.

I look inside and pull out a smartphone. Thing looks crazy expensive on top of it all. "I can't take this."

"I won't hear it. If anything, it will buy me a few years from lack of heart attacks every time you fall out of my sight."

I turn it on and feel like a little kid with a new toy. He has already changed the background to that of a heroic knight slaying a dragon. I laugh. "That's so stereotypical. Why does it always have to be some poor dragon that gets gutted?"

"Well like hell I'm going to let some big lizard eat me..."

I laugh again and hug him. "Okay, but I'm still siding with the dragon."

He hugs me back, and I feel a wave of guilt threaten to drown me. The guy is even more insane than I am. I might not be the only werewolf in the world, and it's a scary thought. I didn't think they could exist in packs.

"Let's grab some food and head home. Seeing as the bakery is still standing, you're likely still hungry."

"Oh you're horrible," I reply and hit him in the chest, and he counterattacks by pinching my nose. I decide to take everything that has happened in stride. Or more simply, I just can't find the courage right now to confront him with what he did to that horrible demon from my past. I just hope it isn't something that is going to land him in a lot of trouble.

TWENTY-TWO

Then

There is a definition of a perfect day, and I remember it still. It's sitting by the outdoor pool with your feet in the freezing cold water. It's listening to the birds chirp in the trees only a few meters away. It's relaxing in the sunlight as it dries out your long, brown hair, and wondering what's for dinner. It's looking at your shoulder as a butterfly lands on it, and hearing your girlfriend say something about being 'blessed' because of it. It's finding yourself pondering that idea in its depth for a majority of the remaining afternoon. It's listening to all of your friends laughing behind you, talking about nothing important but something funny. It's being randomly grabbed from behind and thrown into the water for the crime of daydreaming.

Okay, so maybe sunbathing would have to wait. I

could live with that.

I lifted my head out of the water and rested my arms on the side of the pool to where my almost-boyfriend laughed at me. "Was that necessary?"

"I was just saving you from being so spaced-out," Tristan says.

If I didn't have such a paralyzing crush on the guy along with half the girls my age in my apartment building, I would have chased him down till he went crying to his mother. I was just another piece of the joke that never grew old— throwing people in the pool when they least expect it. I looked away from Tristan's light brown eyes that hid under his brown bangs to see where Jackson sat quiet and shivering amid the group. He was still learning how to swim, but that hadn't stopped his mom from throwing him in the deep end the other day. Necessity often brings out the best in us, particularly when it's to avoid drowning.

Jackson smiles when I sniffle as some water had gone up my nose, and I glared at him expecting him to be laughing behind his dark brown eyes. Everyone had been trying to drag him into the water that day, and they were failing miserably. He was in many ways the opposite of Tristan, not just because he was black, but how he was always empathetic and smarter than his years. Of course, he was, us Virgos are naturals. Tristan, on the other hand, could be as cold and jagged as broken ice, with the ego of an elephant. I had known them both since before I was born as my mother had once been their mother's friend. Now, my mom did everything she could to avoid going outside, and I absentmindedly accepted that. But it was okay because I wasn't alone. In fact, I think at that point in time I was feeling rather overcrowded, and thoroughly soaked.

I look up as the lifeguard blows the whistle for the pool closing and I haul myself out of the deep end. The water was always cold, and now I would have to go home soaked. My mother would be thrilled.

I pick up my towel and found that it too was dripping wet, as my splashdown had soaked it. Wrapping myself as best I could, I waddle out of the outdoor pool like drowned duck and head towards my building.

"Did you want to borrow my towel?" Jackson asks. Naturally, his towel was completely dry.

"I'm fine," I reply with a stubborn shiver.

"Are you coming outside after?" Tristan asks as he heads towards the building's side stairwell.

"I'll try," I answer and continued my waddle to the back entrance, as my girlfriends have already darted off to Samantha's house.

I get off the elevator on the seventeenth floor and say bye to Jackson who still had to travel up to the twenty-fourth floor. On reaching my apartment, I knock, and no one answers. Pulling up my key that was pinned to my towel, I opened the door and revel in the empty apartment, as I now had plenty of time to get dry, write a note, and run out of the apartment again. My social life was a full-time job for me at the time.

After I had changed, I made my way back down to the first floor, where everyone was hanging out at Samantha's house still. I didn't remember how hungry I was until I saw the pizza boxes on the table. After asking, I took a couple slices and then followed Samantha as she called me into the hallway and we sat down. "What's up?" I ask, finding that the look on her face was questionable.

"Nothing." She shrugs, and some of her tight, dark curls fall over her shoulder. "I was just wondering if you and Tristan were a thing now?"

I nearly choke on my pizza, but I quickly regain myself.

"So it's true? I knew it!"

"I...uh... We're just friends." And the blush on my face was just from the spicy pepperoni.

"Well, you should go out with him. I did for a while."

Suddenly any appetite I had left vanished entirely. "You did?"

"Mhm. He's really cute, and it's clear that he likes you."

"Because he threw me in the pool...?"

Sam lets out a frustrated sigh, as if unable to deal with how clueless I was.

I laugh as she was too easy to frustrate out of a conversation. Though, I really didn't want to tell her what my real dilemma was. If she had been watching me that closely, she should have noticed it herself. For every bit of attention that Tristan gave me, Jackson made his interests known without the hurtful teasing. Which should have made my decision easy if my mother didn't hate black people so much.

It was my turn to let out a long sigh. On remembering the boy crew waiting for me outside, I get to my feet. "You just reminded me that I promised to play hockey. You want to come along?"

"I don't think so," Sam replies and gets to her own feet. "Why you like playing hockey so much is beyond me."

"It's fun," I reply. "I'll catch you later then, and thanks for the pizza!" I didn't hear her response as the stairwell's door and her world of gossip, makeup and designer clothes closed behind me.

❀ ❀ ❀

I play street hockey that evening until we couldn't see much of anything anymore in the darkness, and then bid

Tristan and Jackson goodbye, along with the other guys who had come to play as well. It never bothered any of them that a girl played hockey with them and I had never stopped to think that it might until Sam had brought it up. Was it that I fit in as a tomboy? Or that our friendship made saying no to me a taboo? Or was it that I was half decent to have on the team? I guess I will never know. It had turned dark already when I reached my apartment and knocked, and my mother opened the door with an unmistakable volatile shakiness in her eyes. I had arrived home for the last time, and for the worst beating in my life.

TWENTY-THREE

Now

My breakfast is running out the door in a basket by the time I'm awake enough to smell its existence. I find Caleb on the couch, tying his gray running shoes.

"Morning."

"Why did Noah run away with my food?" My voice nearly cracks to the point of sounding like I'm going to cry.

Caleb gives me a big smile. "He has some evil plan cooked up for us on the beach."

"Oh no. You hate water, don't you?"

"Yep."

"You think he's going to force you to learn how to

swim?"

"Yep," Caleb replies. "I could seriously use your services as a superhero today. I don't want to drown. Even if I should with how mad you've been at me."

I have been overly angry at him. But it hurt much more to have him avoid home for so many days. "Sorry."

"Nope, I deserve it. I took advantage of you, and I could have treated you better, starting by having never lied to you. I know my excuses can only sound pathetic at this point, but all of the girls I've have been with these last years have been nothing to me. Most of them were just looking for a partner with money or a good time. None of them was anything like you."

I smile as Caleb's face does look genuinely remorseful.

"I want us to be the way we started as. You are my best friend in this world, and I want you to be happy. It's not my place to interfere if you find that you're happier with someone else. I'm just asking for another chance."

I nod as I can't seem to find anything to say.

"So are you going to get dressed, or do I have to get you dressed?" Caleb asks with a sneaky grin.

I turn red at the thought of Caleb pulling a Noah act on me and disappear into the bedroom to get dressed on my own. Sure enough, I find the blue bathing suit waiting for me on Caleb's bed. I suck up my courage and put it on, and my shorts and T-shirt over it. I'm fighting chickening out now, as the thought of Caleb's reaction to what I look like terrifies me. His voice calls for me to hurry up, and I force myself forward.

Noah has the car started up already downstairs, and Caleb stuffs himself into the back while I take shotgun. It's not too long of a drive to the beach, and it's a beautiful, sunny day to boot. We set up camp near the water, and I quickly realize that Noah has chosen a rather crowded beach. Meanwhile, Caleb is looking at the water like a demon will spring loose and drag him in at any moment. I vow to tie Noah up for the whole day if he forces him into the water. There are things Noah doesn't know or understand when it comes to water and Caleb. And it's not my place to say anything about it. That and I have my own problems. I wonder how fast I can sprint to the deeper part of the water before anyone sees that I'm a scarred monster.

With Noah setting up base and Caleb counting his lives with each wave, I take my shorts and shirt off and make a mad dash for the water. Caleb's eyes don't miss a beat of my escape, and I watch the shore from the safety of the water that I'm now hidden in. Too fast, too furious for the win. No one is getting this mermaid. I watch as Caleb looks to exchange a few words with Noah, who's looking to catch a tan first before hitting the water. Caleb soon resorts to pacing back and forth on the shore in his swim trunks. I have no problem watching his sculpted body all day should he never come in. Meanwhile, I'm perfectly content to play with the waves, while I watch Caleb test the limits of his fear of water.

I'm decidedly cruel and come a bit more into the shallow end. He's not too far away, but still not close enough as he eyes me like his chosen conquest. Caleb takes a few more steps in, before hesitating as a big wave makes the water deeper for a moment.

"You just wait until I catch you..." he playfully warns.

I've only started with him as I swim back and forth, humming, in tune to his pacing on land.

Caleb is getting discouraged, and of course, that causes me to swim closer. He matches me and moves a little deeper. He has the advantage of being tall, which means I have to swim further out to get him submerged. When he's deep enough with the water reaching his chest, I swim over to him. He catches me like I'm a crazed fish and I laugh.

"Now I got you," he says and refuses to let me go as he holds me close.

I can't splash or break free of him, and my laughing is making me weaker. "Hey, you're out here to learn how to swim, not pick up women!"

"Swimming can wait," he says seductively and looks to want to kiss me.

But my eyes aren't on him now, as I look at the beach

where Noah seems to be conversing with their parents. "Oh no."

Caleb looks back to the beach and sees what I do. He slowly and reluctantly lets go of me. "If this is part of Noah's plan, I will kill him."

"I think they're going away. Shhh, don't stare," I tell Caleb and wade out a little further. "Looks like you're going to have to swim after all," I taunt.

Caleb is measuring the height of the waves, and I can see fear on his face. "How do I know you won't let me drown?"

"Um, I won't, but he might," I say as I point to behind Caleb.

Noah comes like a shark out of the water and launches himself at Caleb. He drags him underwater with him.

Caleb comes up gasping for air and shoves Noah away rather angrily. "You prick!" Caleb snaps.

"Hey, if you want to stand here all day, I don't care. But you're boring Aubree," Noah says.

"Noah! you didn't have to do that," I say as I swim over to them.

"Well, he's less scared of the water now," Noah replies, completely heartless to the whole topic.

"Unreal," I say, and I start making my way back to

shore. When we're all sitting on dry sand again, I set a towel over Caleb and rub him dry a bit. He's taking the whole traumatized by water thing rather well. I think. I look for the sunblock, and on finding it, I kneel before him and start to rub a bit on his face. He starts to come around, and his beautiful brown eyes focus on me again. It's only when his eyes are locked on me do I remember my scars. As if reading my mind, Noah takes my towel for himself before I can turn to grab it. "Hey! Are you going to be an ass all day?"

"Maybe," Noah replies, making my towel into a pillow before lying back on it and closing his eyes.

"What's mom and dad doing here?" Caleb asks.

"I don't know, but they sounded like they weren't saying something," Noah replies.

"Huh." Caleb takes his towel off and rubs me dry a bit before wrapping me protectively in it. "They aren't that bad."

I don't need to ask what he's talking about now.

"I should have been there to protect you," Caleb says.

"It's fine. Neither of us had the power to do much of anything back then."

"Well, fortunately, that has changed."

Caleb's arms catch me in an embrace, and he pulls me close, before snatching the sunblock and contently starting to cover me in it. I don't fight him off, as he's taking care of just where he touches. Meanwhile, Noah is seemingly asleep. After a few moments, it feels like someone is watching us and I let my eyes scan the beach. To my surprise, their parents are camped out on the beach, almost out of reach of my sight.

"They're still here, aren't they?" Noah asks.

"Yeah, and watching us," I say as I look away before they can spot me staring.

"Better let go of my fiancé then," Noah suggests.

"Or we could just tell them the truth," Caleb replies, irritated. "Why are they here, anyways?"

"I should have killed that son of a bitch," I say.

Caleb looks at me in worry that I might spring off and pounce on some unsuspecting beachgoer and maul them.

"You think he tipped them off?" Noah asks.

"Tipped who off? What's going on?" Caleb asks.

"I ever-so-accidently beat the shit out of a stalker on Noah at the show. His evil plan didn't roll with me, so now I think that maybe he went straight to your parents," I explain.

"Okay then... Scorned lover, I'm to assume? And exploiting your gayness?" Caleb asks Noah.

"Don't say it like you never had any pissed off ex's,"

Noah retorts.

"Yeah, except mine didn't have the potential to make our parents disown us," Caleb replies.

"Hah, until you hooked up with that stripper," Noah mocks.

"Guys, guys, seriously. We need a plan," I insist.

"It's your call, Boss," Noah says. "The truth is going to eventually surface, but if you want to drag it out, I don't care. Caleb is closer to our parents than I am."

I let out a long sigh as I weigh the situation. "If we call it quits here, they will never trust you again," I tell Noah. "Even if the truth does come to light, you can say in your argument that you tried."

"Aubree, you don't have to do this," Caleb says.

"It's alright. Besides, Noah may as well be a cardboard cutout and not a man."

"Ouch," Noah says in return. "I am here and listening by the way."

"Just vanish for a bit, and I'll make your parents disappear," I plea to Caleb. The need for the two brothers to not go at odds with their parents is important to me. It's likely because I know all too well what it's like to not have any parents at all.

Caleb lets out a long sigh as Noah lifts his sunglasses to

look at him. "I can't believe I'm agreeing to do this..."

Caleb sulks off, and I turn my focus on Noah. Only, I didn't think this far ahead. Reminding myself that Noah isn't a threat, I climb on top of him and kiss him. It's completely random and spontaneous to deal with the situation, but I'm not prepared for when he kisses me back. He doesn't stop there either, as his hands touch my back and nearly break my concentration on the part where this is supposed to be an act. I hit the breaks and pull away when it feels like I might be raping him. I climb off him and give an inconspicuous glance to where his parents had been camped out on the beach, and see that they're packing up and leaving. "Phew. They're going."

Noah sits up and almost looks disappointed, as if I woke him from some happy dream and left him stranded in a less-appealing reality.

"Sorry about going crazy there. I kinda fell too far into character. But it worked," I'm blushing uncontrollably.

"Yeah..." Noah says and looks to find his parents gone. "That was one hell of an act. To think I was siding with the women who claim raping a guy is impossible."

I'm completely red now and embarrassed that I might have gone too far with Noah. What didn't feel that crazy to me seems to have broken something in him. "Sorry again. You going to be alright?"

Noah gives me a look of uncertainty.

TWENTY-FOUR

Now

I can hear Noah and Caleb talking, and I glance at the clock on the dresser for the time. It's 4 am. I yawn and sit up as if my body has woken up automatically from not having Noah nearby.

"She's been broken by enough guys. I don't intend to hurt her."

I tune into the conversation in the living room and lie back down lest they find me awake and listening. I sleep like the dead on any given day. It's likely that they think there isn't any chance of me being awake.

"And just what do you know about being raped and molested? She's mine because I know exactly how she feels right now. Just as I knew her every thought when we were kids. The only thing to every violate you growing up was a golden spoon up your ass."

I hide further under the covers, fearing that I may have unintentionally started a war between them. It hurts to hear them fighting. It hurts more to be the center of it.

"Go ahead and hit me, if that's the only way you think you can win," Caleb says, provoking Noah.

"You don't seem to get that Aubree isn't the one you throw back. You say she's like you, and yet you've only been capable of sleeping around like it's a game of numbers."

"Oh, and just how many have you tossed back, Noah?"

"Of women, none."

"Well so much for your experience in that department," Caleb retorts.

"I'm betting that I could make her happier than you. After all, none of your women stuck around long."

"You're nothing but a selfish bastard, and you make me sick because you know full well that you are one. To think that all my life I always took second place when I was up against you. Because you were the real son, and I was just hitching a ride through the comfortable life. Every time you wanted something I stood back and let you take it. Then you go and find my girl with the whole story of how you did it for me, and yet you take her for yourself anyways. Well, I'm sorry, but I'm not going to stand aside this time. Either you remind her that she's a woman and not some doll in your collection, or I will. And there's not a damn thing you can do to stop me." Caleb storms out of the apartment then, slamming the door behind him.

I'm sitting up again by reflex as I'm scared. Fights have the effect of putting me instantly on edge.

Noah comes into the dark bedroom, and I look at him as a flicker of light passes his green eyes from something outside the window. "I'm sorry you heard that."

"I just wish I wasn't the reason you guys were fighting."

Noah sits next to me on his bed, with his fingers woven together before him. "I knew he was going to lose his patience eventually, but ultimately I have my parents to thank for forcing all of this on us sooner."

"Is everything alright with them? Do they suspect anything?"

"Yeah, you can say that. They're mad because someone said something, and all I have to go on now is my ex you confronted at the show."

"So how do we fix it?" I ask.

"I never intended to marry you for real. I thought we could help each other. I give you a helping hand out of your unfortunate situation, and I end up banking on it.

But this has become something else. That's why I have to know if you still love Caleb before I do anything else."

"Noah..."

"I thought about it, Aubree. Just taking you and running away from all of this," Noah says, looking around. "But I'm not like you. I can't just change my path in life whenever I want. I'm not as free as you are. I wouldn't know what to do with that kind of freedom if I had it."

"You don't have to explain anything. I understand what you're saying. Your world is different, and I've accepted that."

He catches my face with his hand now, and then gently sets me back down against the bed. I don't fight him as he has already crippled all of my defenses. I can feel his sweet breath against my skin. His hands explore me, while his eyes watch my own for some signal to stop. I touch him in turn, and the feel of his chiseled chest under my fingers feels like detailed a map of where my hands should go next. He falls closer to me. Noah's touch is gentle and patient, and it frightens me as I can't bring myself to believe that it's real. He kisses me on the lips, then works his way down my neck, and my entire body burns up with a heat I've never felt. I wonder if this is what I did to him on the beach, and he's just doing this to wake me up to the reality of what I did to him. His hand stops at my lower half, and I have an idea as to why as I wasn't so wet before all of this. I can feel his lower half rise against my body too, as whatever had him immune to me before, isn't working anymore. Noah has melted me into a blissful state of nothingness with just his hands and eyes. What he does to me now doesn't matter; my mind will be lost for days in trying to figure out how to recover from this. His hands come to my sides, and he keeps me pinned under him in the darkness.

"I used to think that the only thing that was important was keeping face and money, but I would be lying if I didn't tell you that I started questioning both the moment I met you. Suddenly the whole love thing began to make some kind of sense, and I didn't care about anything else. I love you, more than anyone I've ever known," Noah says, as his hand brushes back my hair, trying to coax my mind back from its state of bliss to his eyes. "And nothing will ever change that. Even if I have to accept that I'm not the right man for you."

I want to say something in turn, but I'm still helplessly paralyzed.

"I'm going to be gone for a few days to get some connections together for work. I intend to take what I have and move forward, whether my parents approve with their money or not. I know I still sound selfish, but I want you to stay with us. Even if that means choosing Caleb over me. I just can't..." Noah trails off for a moment, looking for the right words. "I just can't see you being with some stranger. It would hurt too much. Hell, I would go mad just worrying about you all the time." Noah is on his feet then and heading for the door.

I spring up from the bed and catch his arm, fearing that he might never come back. I'm crying now, and there isn't anything I can do to stop it. He pulls me into a tight hug and kisses my hair.

"I'll be back. Don't go tearing down the city in the meantime or anything crazy. Caleb can't keep up with you like I can."

I smile and hug him tighter, before forcing myself to let go of his arm. "Put the red cape away for the weekend, got it. But you have to promise me something in return."

"Name it," he replies, confident that he can handle whatever challenge I drop on the table before him. If anything, he's welcoming the idea that I would make it that easy.

"If you see any more crazy ex's, give me at least a phone call. That last one was freaky as hell, and I'll go crazy worrying about you too."

"Alright, I'll text you every day. That way we can keep tabs on each other. Don't lose the phone I gave you and be good," he says and pokes me hard in the center of my forehead, before gathering up his duffle bag and jacket and leaving.

I feel like he just pushed a button to try and make me a child again, but I can never go back to who I was. I'm crying again before the door can so much as close, and it's something out of my control. My head is spinning every which way, made worse by the fact that I also know that everything I have ever tried to hold tightly onto I have lost. I just refuse to accept it.

TWENTY-FIVE

Now

Noah doesn't leave me completely defenseless, as I've been watching his cooking like a hawk. And it's a good distraction as I'm going borderline crazy with him away. I remember just about everything he does to make my pancakes, and when I look at the door, I see that Caleb has just walked in to be my first test mouse.

"Oh no. You sure you know what you're doing over there?" he teases as he hangs his rugged suede jacket up. He doesn't seem to know yet that I heard his fight with Noah last night.

"You tell me," I say and hand him a plate, with the same amount of syrup he always put on.

He hesitates, but sits down at the bar and picks up his

knife and fork. He takes a bite and nods his head in approval. "Not bad. I forgot that you learn quickly."

"Heh, thanks. I forgot that I was a good mimic. We should like watch superhero movies all night so I can mimic them too. I still have to learn how to fly and super-speed, after all."

Caleb laughs and finishes off his pancakes. "Just don't go learning any super-strength moves. The only thing I have over you is physical strength."

I smile and start to clean up the kitchen. I have inadvertently covered a good part of it in flour and sugar. Then I retreat to the living room with my coffee.

"So what are we doing today, Boss?"

It sounds funny when Caleb says it, as I watch him sit on the sofa next to me and turn on the sports channel. His relaxed aura still reaches me, just like when we were kids. I'd be the cat with my hair up and claws in the ceiling, and he'd be the one catching me. "I'm not sure. You don't have work?"

"Nope, I'm all yours."

I take a sip of my coffee as I ponder the things to do outside of the house. I know Caleb enough to know he's not a house mouse by nature. I have to pull my fading childhood memories forward to get ideas. "You know what we have never done? Played street hockey."

"I remember you mentioning something about that. But there was just too much grass and gravel at our foster home."

"I know. You have two sticks by chance?"

"Finish your coffee, and I'll go find them. And wear something that I can illegally tackle you in."

I'm laughing now as I know Caleb is dead-serious. He's even bolder than I remember him. But then again, so am I. I want to accuse him of pushing my feelings for Noah aside in my heart, but I can't. I can't because Caleb has always been there, taking up much of its space. I turn the TV off and slip into the bedroom, and get dressed in a pair of skinny jeans and a light sweater. Noah has left me a small pile of clothes on the chair, and I feel even more babied. He sees me as completely helpless on an average day without him around. I reluctantly have to agree that he's partially right.

"Aubree!"

I hear Caleb call for me and leave the apartment, locking it behind me, and head downstairs. He has the beat-up car warmed up, and I jump in shotgun.

"I'm thinking the park a few blocks away, the one with the basketball courts?"

"Sounds good," I reply, and we're off.

We get there, and I help unpack the sticks while he

takes the small hockey bag with the shin pads and gloves. I put the gloves on as he sets up a couple tiny pylons for the net at the end of the basketball court. I punch my gloves together, ready for a fight. I lift up my hockey stick and aim for him. Meanwhile, my head is telling me that I'm totally screwed, and he's going to turn me into the orange ball on this court. I put the ball down on the concrete, and make a dash for the net.

He's ready to intercept, but I spin around him, tapping the ball through his legs and between the pylons. He's too tall for his own good.

"So that's how it's going to be, eh?" he says, as takes the ball to the other end as I go on defense.

I may as well be a stain on the floor with how fast he gets past me and scores. But now I'm mad as I take the ball to the other end. I make it halfway across the court, and spotting my opening, send it hurling his way with a slap-shot. It goes past him as he scrambles out of the way, and between the pylons.

"Hey, you're not allowed to be rough!" he tells me as he gets the ball and we switch sides again.

We play until we're sweaty and exhausted, then we head to the grass just outside the court. Caleb collapses to the ground, and I sit next to him. "Well, I got my exercise quota in for the year."

"Silly lightweight," he says and tosses some grass at me.

I'm too exhausted to fight back, but I still poke his ticklish side. He jerks back and then retaliates by trying to grab my arm. I'm too quick as I scramble backward. He springs at me and tackles me to the grass before I can get to my feet. I'm laughing too hard now as he pins me there, wearing his conquest grin. "Not fair."

"You started it."

"Uh huh,' I reply, unconvinced. "Not my fault you're still ticklish. Granted, I had to be sure."

He falls to the grass next to me and is now playing with the ends of my long brown hair as if contemplating what he's going to do next. We become content with each other's quiet company, till his brown eyes focus on mine more intently.

"I remember your hair being lighter."

"The sun tends to bleach it," I say. I haven't been getting much of it till now.

"And those eyes," he continues, tracing the top of my brow with his finger. "They're green today. Always changing."

"I'm content. At least, I think green means I'm content." I feel like a kid again, as Caleb watches me, trying to see what I'm thinking. My eyes aren't telling him enough.

"I wish I was older back then. To think that I lost you

for so many years."

I can feel a genuine hint of sadness in his voice, and I know that I feel the same way. "Hey, it worked out for the better."

"It worked out for me. But you're the one who had to suffer."

"Hey, don't get all sappy on me. Sometimes you have to deal with the bad so you can see how important the good things are."

"Maybe," he says and is tugging at my bangs now. "There aren't a lot of days I can remember where I didn't think about you at least once. I thought I could move on if I found a way to forget about you, but I never could. Now I don't have to anymore."

The sunlight has his blond hair glowing, and I remember what he looked like when he was younger. Time may move forward, but it's not that good at covering its tracks. He looks much like his younger self, just more likely to devour me and ask questions later this round. His hands are rougher, but they have the same gentle touch. The back of my mind is reminding me that I'm likely the bottom of the list of all the women he's had and would likely remain such if dared to try and take him again. I would just make an embarrassing failure of myself. I was a stray dog chasing squirrels. I wouldn't know what to do if I caught him. Yet he would always be the top of my list, even if my fate had been different and I had some semblance of a normal life after we parted. It seems so unfair.

"What are you thinking about?" he asks.

"I'm thinking about that deer that surprised us when we were in the hunting perch in that tree."

"Heh, that was a surprise. It was like right under us. You were scared as if it were some baby bear cub that would have its mother charging at us at any moment."

"Hey, those antlers are sharp. I wasn't going to climb down and pet it and then explain just what I was doing to its mother. I could barely keep you from doing just that."

"You were always watching my back, even then."

My body is tenser now than I want it to be when he touches my face. Noah has the uncanny ability to disable me with a single touch, yet with Caleb, I'm on the defensive, and I can't pin exactly why. Maybe I'm trying to protect him from all of my failures. From my curse that destroys everything and everyone around me. He senses my unease and rolls onto his back in defeat.

I sit up and shake the blush away and start brushing the grass off of me. Caleb decidedly closes his eyes as if to take a nap. "And you call me a lightweight..."

He smiles in reply, but I know he's not saying something. He wants me, even if he won't say it outright. I fear that I'm hurting him by pushing him away all the while taking advantage of having both him and Noah, all because I can't beat into my thick skull that they deserve someone better and to stop leading them on. Someone who isn't as messed up and as useless as me. I lie back down, resting my head on Caleb's stomach. He doesn't seem to mind as he sets his hand down on my hair. His breathing calms me down, and I close my eyes, counting his heartbeats. Falling from grace is so much harder than getting there. I feel as if another part of me understands what Noah said to me, and I cling onto Caleb's shirt by reflex.

TWENTY-SIX

Now

I can feel Caleb eyeing me like a predator, and I'm worried that he's not going to stop. We've decided to downtime our day by taking on the superhero movies, and I'm wondering if I can keep him at body-length from me as he makes several long glances from the TV my way. He's just waiting for the moment to catch me off-guard, as he tests my attention level by pulling my toes. That and I would have to be blind to completely ignore the fact that he's in my line of sight.

He's such a contrast to Noah that it's enough to spend half a lifetime pondering over. Noah calculates everything, is organized and is usually predictable. Caleb is wild, completely unpredictable and an opportunist opposed to a planner. And he has always been fun to be around. It makes him a hundred times more dangerous, as I can feel his hands move up my calves in a caress. He's testing me and doesn't seem to know that if it weren't for my million inner demons, I would have been all over him already from hormonal overload. I can't keep myself from smiling at him now, and he has his whole focus on me now. My phone vibrates in the chest pocket of the shirt I stole from Caleb, and I get up to text back the only person it can be. Noah.

I don't get far into the kitchen once I've texted back when Caleb catches me exactly where he wants. He comes up from behind me and spins me around, before lifting me onto the counter like I weigh nothing. He has his hands on my back now as he pulls me closer and kisses me, which is almost enough to disarm me as I take in the look in his eyes. He's hungry, and all my denial in the world can't stop me from feeling the same when he kisses me harder. We are both are so caught up in each other's touch, that the hit to the door has to come twice before we hear it.

Caleb is upset now from being interrupted, as he goes over to the door and asks who it is. His answer is a kick against the door that shatters the locks off of the frame. Another kick whips open the door, and two large men are on Caleb before he can defend himself.

My hand is on the kitchen knife on the block just as a terrifyingly familiar face comes straight for me. I hold Jeff at knife point, while he aims his gun at my head.

192

"Silly Aubree. I see you haven't changed," Jeff says with an evil grin. "Now put the knife down, or your little boy toy here gets it."

I half-glance at Caleb who is being held at gunpoint by one of the bald men. They have him gagged and tied to a chair now. I whisper silent curses. Caleb and Noah attacked the right guy, just in the wrong decade as Jeff is clearly part of a gang now.

I move to slowly drop the knife, and Jeff immediately grabs me by the throat and smashes my face against the bar counter. I feel nothing from the hit, as my anger hits a new high.

"I see you've done well for yourself," Jeff says as he keeps me pinned against the bar and glances around. "But you didn't really think you could send your high-class attack dogs after me and not pay the consequences, did you?"

I swear to kill and dismember this demon from my past as all my fury isn't enough to get him off of me. But I have to escape, somehow. Caleb is in danger too. I scan the counter for something I can use as a weapon. Damn Noah's tidiness. There's nothing lying around. I swear and curse and it gets my head pummelled against the counter again before he tears me around to face him, my hair tight in his grasp.

"Feels almost like the old days, don't you think?" he says, laughing as his gang friends do the same.

I'm defeated; as my attempts to escape get me slapped and punched. The back of my broken thoughts screams to just give up and die as he grabs me by the throat and crushes my back against the bar table. His gun takes aim at my heart. At least my end will be quick.

"It's been fun getting back together and all Aubree, but you were more fun in the past." He fires the gun, and it hits, and I collapse as all air and light forsake me.

"What about him?" one of the other men ask.

"We'll ransom him, he's worth something," Jeff says, and I hear his footsteps leave the kitchen as my mind gives up the fight to stay conscious, despite Caleb's desperate cries.

TWENTY-SEVEN

Now

I wonder if this is how Noah's grandfather felt as he lay dying, as I stare at Caleb gagged and tied to a chair across from me, desperately trying to escape his bonds. His wrists are bleeding. I'm dead. At least, I think I am as I don't know of anyone to take a bullet to the heart and live. Caleb is crying, as he stares at the floor. If I am still alive, the room is darker now. It must be nighttime.

I take in a deep breath, and everything in my body burns at once. I thought I could feel and take on all the pain in the world, but this one is crippling. The room is empty of attackers, but my instincts tell me it's not for long. I wiggle, and my fingers respond as my eyes catch something on the bar, showing slightly on the edge. It's the gun that shot me. I feel like I've won the lottery.

I wiggle some more, and get up alongside the leg of the bar counter, before managing to hit it hard enough with my body to knock the gun down. I almost scream in pain as I bring my arm forward to pick it up. I tuck it under my back and return to playing dead. I'm exhausted out of my mind. I refuse to give up. I'm going to kill these bastards for what they did to Caleb and me. Hell can have me for all I care, as long as he's okay.

"It's dark now. Get that body out of here before it starts to stink," Jeff orders.

Two sets of footsteps enter the room. One of the brutes grabs my legs, and the other, my arms. The one with my arms doesn't get a chance to react when I pull the trigger on him, straight at his head. The other drops my legs and pulls his gun on me, and we fire at the same time. His bullet lands in my shoulder, while mine hits him in the chest, sending him falling backward.

One more to go. Jeff comes out of the washroom with his hands up, likely expecting a swat team. I have his gun in my hands.

"Aubree."

I pull the trigger. The shot hits his thigh and sends him to the ground in a cry. He swears as he crawls his way to me to finish the fight. But that only puts his face where I can hit it better. One more shot in his head and he stops moving.

I collapse entirely against the floor as I just don't have the strength to move anymore. I want to tell Caleb that it's going to be alright and how much I love him, but I'm just too tired. I close my eyes and let the darkness take me. I'm not scared to leave the world of the living anymore.

TWENTY-EIGHT

Now

My mother's black hole theory is a lie. It's taken me twenty-five years to realize this. She had told me that it's a place of darkness, where they leave you to rot and never look at you again. I can see now that I'm in this black hole she spoke of, but I can hear everything around me with uncanny clarity.

"Aubree."

It's Noah. He's close, but it feels like he's still so far away.

"Dammit woman, you can't sleep forever. Wake up. It's okay now. Please just wake up."

I obey and open my eyes. His green eyes are watery, and it's clear that he's been crying for some time. "Noah."

"There you are," he says and touches my hair as a smile appears on his face.

"Please tell me I'm not in the hospital again?"

He laughs briefly and looks around. "Sorry, I tried to get you out again, but the cops overpowered me. How are you feeling?"

"Like crap. Where's Caleb? Is he alright?"

"Yeah, he's okay. Though I think he is more shook up than you, despite you being the one to take two bullets."

I turn my head and look at the nightstand where the phone that Noah had given me lies, complete with a bullet stuck in its center. "I'm sorry I broke it."

"Oh, would you give it up? You're alive. That's what's important. A phone can be replaced, but not you," Noah says.

I touch my shoulder where I remember the bullet hitting my shoulder. I contemplate asking Noah to design me a bullet-proof outfit for his next campaign.

Noah pulls my gown down a bit to get a look at the wound himself. "I'm starting to think that you're a magnet for violence and gunshots."

"I think you're right." I try to sit up, but my whole body still feels like it was shattered against a pole by some giant.

200

"Are you hungry? I can't approve of much of the food they have here, but I didn't go home yet." Noah heads over to the rolling table and brings me a tray with some meat and vegetables on it. It's the right serving size for a mouse.

"I'm going to die here," I say as I take it from him.

"Not if I can help it. If you can hold your own here for a bit, I can grab something from home, assuming the cops have stopped marching all over our place."

"That be great," I say as I finish off the meal faster than I could have inhaled it, and he puts the tray back for me.

"Alright, then don't go walking out of here for the next hour. I'll be back quick, okay?"

I nod and watch him go, and the room suddenly feels a lot colder. I look at my vitals on the monitor and watch them for a while until I fall asleep to the whirs and beeps.

❊ ❊ ❊

I don't know how long I'm asleep for when I feel someone staring at me. I open my eyes and instead of Noah, I find a woman staring back down at me. I didn't realize until now that she has the same eyes as Noah, only an icier version. "Mrs. McCowan?"

"Aubree," she replies in monotone.

I instinctively look around for Noah or Caleb, as my instincts scream at me that she's not here for a friendly visit of concern.

"My sons aren't here," she says in answer to my thoughts. "Nor will you be seeing them any longer, as the continuous stream of problems that you bring is now over."

I don't know what she means by never being able to see them again, and I'm now in panic mode as my heart rate causes the monitor to beep faster. "What do you want?"

"In the next few weeks, you're going to be released from this hospital. That's when you need to go back to where you came from."

"And if I tell you to go to Hell?"

"Then along with the assault charges that Noah's ex is willing to lay down on you, I will be charging you with fraud myself. You're going to go to jail, and you're going to be there for quite some time if you refuse."

"Fraud? What the hell are you talking about?" The pain in me is vanishing fast as I start to boil over with anger.

"Oh come on now, Aubree. Did you seriously think that no one would see through your tricks and deceit? It's clear that you pretended to be Noah's fiancé for financial compensation and without any kind of intention to marry him."

I'm laughing now as what she's saying is just unreal. "I never took any money from him."

"Is that so?" Mrs. McCowan says. "Well, the bank account in your name would suggest otherwise. You have a considerable amount in there, considering that you're just a prostitute from the ghetto."

I don't say it, but ouch. I silently object to the prostitute term. Then I promise to strangle Noah for doing something so stupid as getting me a bank account and putting money in it. Count on him to worry too much about me — so much that it lands us both in even hotter water. I lie back down. I give up. I see now why Noah hates this bitch so much.

"Of course, if you return the money and promise to not try and contact Noah or Caleb, all can be forgiven. If for anything, for curing Noah for me."

"Noah was never sick," I snap back at the woman.

"You have until you walk out of here to decide." Then Mrs. McCowan turns and leaves, her red high heels clicking out of earshot.

I feel sick inside from the thought that she likely threatened Caleb and Noah with the same thing — to jail me if they tried to contact me again. I already know that they wouldn't risk it. Their mother has had an iron grip on their lives for too long.

I try to sit up again, but a surge of pain pushes me back down. I'm helpless and weak, and I hate it. I have to see them. I don't care if I go to prison, but I refuse to let them go like this.

TWENTY-NINE

Now

Two weeks go by, and no one comes to visit me. In my heart, I know that it's not Noah's and Caleb's fault, but the loneliness still hurts. I've been spoiled with attention and false affection, and now I have to withstand the sting that is left for being without either. It was a sweet dream, I keep telling myself, but the nightmare is my reality, and nothing can ever change that.

I sit up in my hospital bed as I don't want to lie down and do nothing anymore. If they don't come to me, I know I have to find them, somehow. I don't know how I get out of the hospital, as everything spins madly around me. I'm fuelled solely by instinct and desperation, and perhaps lots of madness, and I hail a cab.

Some minutes later the cab driver tells me that we've

arrived and I pull out my wallet and pay him, before getting out at Caleb and Noah's apartment. I silently thank Noah for the money that my wallet still contains. I make it inside and turn on the lights. The apartment is empty. I walk over to the bedroom and open Noah's drawers, and find them next to empty. I'm too late. She has already taken them.

I sit down on Noah's bed as I feel myself start to cry. I force them back, knowing that I will lose the strength of my rage if I give into despair now. I'm going to lose the only two people who ever really mattered to me. I collapse on Noah's bed and close my eyes. I can still smell his scent on the sheets, and it breaks down the rest of my rage, and my eyes give way to a tsunami of tears. I pull out the phone Noah gave me and study its demise. The glass is cracked all over, and it's slightly bent inwards from the impact. It saved my life, but now I want nothing more than for it to be able to make a phone call. If I called them from this phone, somehow they would answer. A miracle for a miracle. It has to work.

I sit back up and think to my shopping street with the bakery. There was a phone repair sign on my route. I get up and ignore the pain surging through my body as I head back out the door. I walk along the street, staying aware for the store I saw. I find it, and hastily pick up my pace and head inside. It's empty, and I'm grateful as I set the broken phone down on the counter. The man behind it doesn't even get a chance to speak before I start pleading for him to fix it. He seems fascinated by my survival story, but clueless as to how to make the miracle I so desperately need right now.

"I'm sorry ma'am, but there's nothing that I can do for this phone." He turns it over in his hands, then pops out a tiny card that seems intact. "I can put your SIM card into another phone if you like, though. It will have your number and contacts saved."

"Please," I say as I look at the phone models spread out before me. "Will it take to a cheaper one?" I know now that Noah spent a fortune on my phone as I see the price of the same model in the display.

"Sure," he says and pulls out a smaller phone with a smaller screen. He pops the card into it and turns it on, then hands it to me. I fiddle with it a moment to find Noah's and Caleb's number and feel victorious. I return the old broken phone to my pocket and pay, and head out of the store. I don't waste another moment calling Noah's number. It takes several tries, but eventually, Noah picks up the phone. Or at least I hope it's Noah, as there is no response from the other end. "Noah?" I listen closer and hear breathing, and then what sounds like a plane flying overhead. Then the line goes dead. I try Caleb's number, but I get no answer at all. I'm pacing back and forth now in my madness, trying to work out in my head where they could be. I heard a plane, but there are two airports near the city, and I don't have enough money to taxi it to both in hopes of finding them.

"Aubree?"

I jump and spin around at the sound of my own name, and to my surprise, find my father standing there.

"I was hoping I would run into you here. I went to the apartment, but no one was there. Is everything okay?"

If I didn't hate him so much, I might have broken down and spilled all my miseries onto him, but I keep it together. I have to keep the last fragment of my pride intact...for something. "Yeah, I'm just trying to figure out how to get to the airport."

"The airport? Why?"

"My finance's mother is kidnapping him to another country, and I'm seriously lost as to how to try and stop her."

"Seriously? Has that woman gone this far?"

"What do you mean?" I ask, trying to figure out how my father would know anything about the McCowans.

"Let's just say I had an interesting phone call from my lawyer yesterday when this woman tried to take by force the money I gave you out from your account." He pulls out his phone and makes a call then.

I'm speechless as I have my answer to where the money came from. I'm even more lost as to whether I can trust this man called my father, or if this all part of some more devious plot.

"They're at the Kensing Airport."

I follow silently to his blue sports car and get in as he gets into the driver's side. It all seems too easy. Miracles are never this easy for me.

We reach the airport in thirty minutes, and I jump out of the car and speed inside. I dial Noah's number, hoping to track him by the sound of his ringtone. The airport is huge, but I don't lose hope. I'm too close now. If I leave here with nothing else, I want an answer.

I hear the familiar beeping of his ringtone, and take off like a madwoman towards it. I come to a screeching halt soon after when I see Noah, Caleb and their parents standing near a counter. They don't see me and I can't make my legs move closer to them. My phone stops ringing Noah's and I will for him to turn around. Will he see me? Ignore me? Will his mother get between us? "Noah."

It's less than a whisper, but it's loud enough to cut through the noise of the crowded airport, and he turns around and sees me. We stare at each other for what feels like an eternity. He takes a step forward, but his mother senses something amiss and turns around to see me. She grabs his arm and gives me a scorching look.

Mrs. McCowan walks over to me, and I hold my ground. I don't care if she has me arrested here, I'm not afraid of her anymore.

"What are you doing here?" she asks in her usual demanding tone.

I don't answer her. I can't because all I want to do is hit her and it's taking all of me to hold myself back.

She takes out her cell phone and calls what sounds like the cops. Figuring that I'm going to be spending my future in jail, I make a break for Noah. Caleb won't so much as look at me before walking away.

"Aubree, you can't be here. You're still injured too—" Noah says.

"I don't care," I practically squeak as I hug him. "Let her put me in jail. You're right about the whole freedom thing. It seriously sucks, especially when you have no idea what to do with it. But you can't just leave like this."

"I'm sorry. I thought I could break free of my family, if only for you, but I've put you through so much pain." Noah turns his face momentarily away from me. "I don't want to see you in jail or hurt anymore because of me. You have to go."

I'm crying now, and it's weakening my strength. "Will you ever come back?"

"Maybe one day," he says and kisses me on the top of my head. "Be good in the meantime." Then he turns and follows after Caleb and his mother.

I stand there, contemplating chasing after him like a

madwoman until someone touches my arm and distracts me. I turn around and then look way up to find a very tall security guard. I don't put up a fight as he escorts me out of the airport and leaves me outside. My father is next to his car, seemingly waiting for me. I walk over to him.

"Did you find him?" he asks me.

"Yes," I say and look briefly around, fearing the cops will jump and tackle me to the concrete at any moment.

"What did he say?"

"Nothing," I reply. "Can I steal a ride back to the city?"

"Yeah, get in," he says and opens the passenger side of the door for me.

I figure I must look too broken and out of it to open my own doors anymore and get into the car.

THIRTY

Now

I don't know why I choose to keep torturing myself, but I stay for the next week at Caleb's and Noah's place. I don't take up my father's offer to stay with him, as he seems unusually helpful and it's unnerving. I've never trusted anyone who just offers help without wanting something in return. They always want something in return, and I've yet to figure out just what my father hopes to gain from me.

I'm packing my knapsack with the few sets of clothes that I now own and head over to the kitchen. I stuff into my bag a few munchies for the road and swing it over my shoulder. I don't know where I'll go, I just know that I'll go mad if I stay here thinking about Noah and Caleb around the clock like some mad woman.

I just make it to the door when it opens from the other side. I step back and look to find Caleb standing there. I'm not sure what to say, as he still has that defeated look on his face. I can't bring myself to think that he might blame himself for what happened. Is he here because he feels sorry for me? Did he forget something important? Is he here to kick me out? I have a million questions and not an ounce of courage to ask any of them.

"Hey," he says, and looks down at me.

I feel like a lost mouse who has just been caught.

"You headed out?" he asks, seeing my knapsack.

"Yeah, I figured I should. Did you come back from your trip early?"

"I didn't want to stay any longer. I was worried about you," Caleb says.

"I'm fine," I lie. I've missed him too much. "Is Noah with you?"

"He chose to stay with our parents." Caleb comes inside and closes the door behind him, before leaning against it. "Before I say anything else, I wanted to apologize."

"For what?"

"I couldn't save you when you needed me the most. Not now or back then. What that monster did to you —"

"Caleb, stop. It's over now, and none of it was your fault," I say, wishing that he would stop beating himself up over it.

"I should have been able to protect you, but instead I brought the monsters down on us. Jeff. My parents. Heck, even Noah and his misplaced sense of reality."

"Your brother isn't misplaced," I insist.

"I wanted to believe that too, but he isn't here."

"Not everyone can take on the world like how we do. Noah told me that he wouldn't know what to do with freedom if he had it, and I believe him, so I don't blame him for staying behind with your parents. Heck, look how long it took me to get out of my crappy life scenario. I'm not the sweet little Aubree you remember. I didn't get the happily ever after ending. I got the one where you turn into a monster and wait for someone to put you down."

"You're not a monster. I promised to come back for you, and I was too late. That doesn't mean I have to let you go now."

"Why me?" I ask, looking at him for a straight answer. "You can have any woman you want."

Caleb looks at the window on the other side of the room and then back at me. "Because my feelings for you never changed. And I won't lie, I tried to move on. I've seen other women, and I've tried to forget you. But I don't think fate is going to let that happen anytime soon. Let me take care of you."

I look away from him as the look on his face hurts my frozen heart. "I can't be a part of your world, Caleb. I will never fit into this lifestyle. Even if I somehow could, I would be too messed up for it."

"Who says we have to live like this?"

"Yet I would never drag you down to my level. I'm sorry, Caleb, but I'm tired. Just forget about me and go."

"I'm not going anywhere, and neither are you," Caleb says and walks over to me. He takes my knapsack off and then heads to the bedroom where he sets it down. Then he comes back to the living room and sits down on the sofa.

I go over to him and sit next to him, before leaning my head against his shoulder. He pats my head, and I instantly feel better.

"So you coming to work with me tomorrow?" he asks, lightening up the air between us.

"Seriously? You want me near your cars?"

"Well, just in case Noah's ex decides to carry out his threat and have you charged, we have our choice of getaway cars."

I laugh as I think about the Beetle that Caleb had to deal with at work, and wonder if I could even fit him into such a small car. "I want the pink Beetle."

"Oh hell no. I burning that car just to make sure, first thing tomorrow." He pulls me into his arms, and I feel helpless as I stare up at his protective gaze on me. "I'm thinking one of our trucks."

"Nope. I want the Beetle."

"Why that horrible thing?" Caleb asks.

"Because just in case I crash into everything, it's perfectly shaped to roll me out of trouble."

"No way you're driving," he says.

I laugh, and he holds me tighter.

"I love you too much, you know that?"

The word 'love' hits me unexpectedly, and I'm left speechless.

"I know that you care deeply about Noah," Caleb continues, seemingly mustering all his courage together to get it out, "but I know I can make you love me more. If you give me a chance."

I close my eyes and press my face against his shirt. His heart beats so fast that his body feels overheated from its effort. I never fell out of love with you. But I can't say it. My heart is different now. There's someone else holding it hostage, and my voice is imprisoned in silence.

My whole body ignites to instantly match his temperature. The desire in his eyes for me are locked within their own prison. Fearful. I don't know if it's his own past and demons that he's scared to let through, or if it's just the thought of taking something from his brother. I want nothing more than to pull every last one of his demons from him and into the heat of the fire that ignites between us when we're together. I close my eyes as I feel time come to a standstill around us again. We've become lost in it. Lost as we may be, neither of us are broken anymore. As long as we're together, we're unbreakable.

ABOUT THE AUTHOR

Sylvia Aer has been writing since she got her first typewriter at eleven. She has worked in graphic design and publishing fields. When she's not writing or working, she can be found baking, reading, or listening to music.

www.ingramcontent.com/pod-product-compliance
Lightning Source LLC
Chambersburg PA
CBHW020409210626
46816CB00006BB/2202